Thad couldn't look away from her, his chest buzzing with warmth and compassion for this brave, beautiful woman who'd stepped in when no one else could.

First for her sister, then with him. They were close now, so close her warm breath fanned his face. He heard her breath catch and saw her pink lips part, and his long-dead heart jumped with excitement, swelling bigger in his constricted chest until he thought he might die from sheer anticipation. He closed his eyes, whether to sear this memory into his brain or because it felt like too much, too soon, he wasn't sure. He whispered her name like a prayer, "Emma."

Then suddenly they were kissing. He wasn't sure who leaned into whom, but Thad couldn't get enough. He cupped her cheeks, her skin silky and hot beneath his fingertips. Emma stilled at first, then clutched his shirt in her fist, right over his heart, keeping him right where he was. Time slowed and the world narrowed to only them, only now, only this kiss.

Dear Reader,

When coming up with story ideas for a new holiday book, I try to go back to the movies and TV shows I loved most as a kid. And one of my all-time favorites (even now) is the Dr. Seuss classic *How the Grinch Stole Christmas!* I wondered how I could take that original concept and make it Harlequin Medical Romance–worthy—and also add more heart and depth and romance for the characters. Thus, Thad and Emma's fairy-tale Manhattan love story was born!

My grumpy hero, Dr. Thad Markson, begins as a bit of a talented, mad hermit. Avoiding everyone and only focused on his work. But the sunshine heroine, nurse Emma Trudeau, has other plans and is determined to recruit the man everyone at the hospital has nicknamed the Grinch of Fifth Avenue into helping her make one sick little boy's wishes come true. Together, they both rediscover the magic of the holidays and the blessing of true love, too.

I do hope you enjoy this winter wonderland romantic confection of a story, and I wish you and yours the very best and brightest of the season.

Until next time, happy reading!

Traci <3

A MISTLETOE KISS IN MANHATTAN

TRACI DOUGLASS

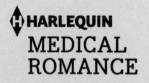

HARLEQUIN

MEDICAL
ROMANCE

HARLEQUIN®
MEDICAL
ROMANCE™

Recycling programs
for this product may
not exist in your area.

ISBN-13: 978-1-335-73747-2

A Mistletoe Kiss in Manhattan

Harlequin Enterprises ULC
22 Adelaide St. West, 41st Floor
Toronto, Ontario M5H 4E3, Canada
www.Harlequin.com

Printed in U.S.A.

Traci Douglass is a *USA TODAY* bestselling romance author with Harlequin, Entangled Publishing and Tule Publishing, and has an MFA in Writing Popular Fiction from Seton Hill University. She writes sometimes funny, usually awkward, always emotional stories about strong, quirky, wounded characters overcoming past adversity to find their forever person. Heartfelt, healing happily-ever afters. Connect with her through her website: tracidouglassbooks.com.

Visit the Author Profile page at Harlequin.com.

To my wonderful editor, Charlotte,
who always has my back.

CHAPTER ONE

DASHING THROUGH THE SNOW...

Emma Trudeau ran from the employee parking lot across the street to the side entrance of Manhattan West General Hospital, unwinding her emerald-green scarf from around her neck. The forecast had been clear earlier in the day, but the weather changed fast in New York City in late November.

She pressed the badge on a lanyard around her neck to the reader beside the door, then pushed inside when the buzzer sounded. A wave of heat and antiseptic scent rushed over her. Hurrying down the well-lit hall toward the front lobby, the soles of her shoes squeaked on the shiny linoleum. For once, Emma wasn't working today in the ER. As charge nurse, she'd picked up more than her fair share of overtime lately for the upcoming holiday season. She rounded the corner at the end of the hall into the spacious lobby area, with its atrium on one side and lots of seating beneath it. A large Christmas tree sat in one corner, adorned with homemade stars from one of the local charities. Kids with disabilities or illnesses that made it hard for them to have happy holidays made them, and people or businesses then chose a wish from the tree to fulfill. Every year, Manhattan West picked one special star to go all out on and this year, Emma was in charge of the project to create the magical wish of one child's dream.

In fact, she was here now—on her day off—to meet with the hospital's chief of staff and the HR director to fill them in on her plans thus far. And she was late.

After passing through security, Emma broke into a near-jog down the long hall toward the other side of the hospital and made it to the small waiting area in front of HR with thirty seconds to spare. She stopped to catch her breath, but before she got the chance an office door opened and the HR director, Jane Ayashi, stuck her head out. "Hi, Emma. Come on in."

Emma tucked her scarf into the pocket of her coat, then smoothed a hand over her long, loose box braids before walking into the office to greet Manhattan West's chief of staff. "Hello, Dr. Franklin."

"Emma," he said. The man was sixty-two if he was a day, but looked at least two decades younger, with a distinct resemblance to Denzel Washington and a deep booming voice like James Earl Jones. "I hope this meeting is worth being late to my granddaughter's Thanksgiving pageant."

"I believe it is, sir. I wanted to let you know my choice of partner on the wish project before the press conference tonight." She took off her coat and draped it over the back of her chair, then sat, her stomach twisting slightly with anxiety. "I think this person will bring a lot to the table."

"Wonderful!" Jane clasped her hands atop her desk. "Are they coming as well?"

Emma's smile faltered. The person she'd chosen wasn't coming to the meeting because Emma hadn't asked them yet. But she would once she got the okay from Jane and Dr. Franklin. She gripped the folder in her lap tighter to hide her shaking fingers. She wasn't nervous, really. Stress was her constant companion working in the fast-paced ER. No, this was more an adrenaline rush. This project was a big deal for her. If she pulled it off well, it could move her to the top of the list for the next big promotion in her department. Meaning more money, more benefits, and hopefully better hours. Now all she had to do was convince the man she wanted working beside her on this project to do it. A difficult task to be sure, considering his reputation around the hospital as the biggest Grinch around. But he had the resources and the clout to grant even the most extravagant wish a kid could ask for, and that's all that was important.

"Uh, no. He won't be here," Emma said, swallowing hard. "In fact, I believe he's upstairs now in surgery."

Dr. Franklin frowned. "Who is it?"

"Dr. Thad Markson."

For a long moment, both Jane and Dr. Franklin just blinked at her, their expressions blank. She began to worry they'd not heard her, but then Dr. Franklin laughed.

"You're joking, right? Dr. Thaddeus Markson? The biggest cardiothoracic surgeon in the city? I'm sorry, Nurse Trudeau, but you better pick someone else. There's no way he's doing this project."

Emma squared her shoulders. "I realize Dr. Markson is a very busy man, but…"

"It's not that," Dr. Franklin chuckled. "Though good luck finding a slot in his surgery schedule. But outside of work, the man's an island. A virtual hermit. Not surprising since he has the charm of an angry polar bear. He'll eat you up and spit you out."

"I think what John is trying to say," Jane said, cutting in, "is that there might be more suitable candidates to work with you on this important project, Emma."

"No. I want Dr. Markson." Emma lifted her chin. "I'm aware of his reputation as being disagreeable toward the staff, but I've done my research and I truly believe he's the best partner for me on this project."

"The Fifth Avenue Grinch? Granting Christmas wishes?" Dr. Franklin managed to get out between guffaws. "He hates the holidays with a passion. I can't imagine his face when you asked him."

Emma had never shied away from a challenge, and she wasn't about to start, not with a possible promotion on the line. She lifted her chin. "He doesn't know yet."

Dr. Franklin sobered fast. "What?"

"I plan to go upstairs after this meeting to talk to him after he's done with his surgery and bring him down to the press conference in the lobby." Emma squared her shoulders. "I just wanted to let you both know first."

"Nurse Trudeau, I've always liked you.

You're smart, hardworking, willing to take on anything we ask of you and do it with a smile," Dr. Franklin said, sitting forward, his expression serious. "But please choose someone else for your partner on this. Trust me as someone who's tried to work with him before. Dr. Markson will only make your life a living hell if you get him involved. He's a brilliant surgeon, but he's awful outside the OR. For a project like this one, you need someone with heart and soul, and there are people who'd deny he has either. I only tolerate him because we need his expertise and the privately funded clients he brings into our teaching hospital."

"I hear what you're saying, Dr. Franklin. I do. But I'm used to dealing with difficult people. Most patients in the ER come to see us at the worst moment of their lives." Emma stood firm in her conviction that Dr. Thad Markson was the right man for her project. He just needed a little nudge in the right direction, a dose of sunshine to light his way. And Emma was nothing if not an optimist. "He'll be my partner. Don't worry. Just give me time."

"The wish project must be completed on Christmas Eve," Jane reminded her. "That's only a month away."

"I know. And that's why I want Dr. Markson working with me on this. We need the wealthy donors and connections he can add to this project to make whatever wish our sick child wants granted a reality in such a short time."

Several beats stretched out in silence, until finally, Dr. Franklin shook his head. "You are persistent, aren't you, Nurse Trudeau? I still think it's risky, if not impossible, but maybe he'll say yes just to get you out of his hair."

Now it was Emma's turn to laugh. "Maybe. Just call me Cindy Lou Who."

Jane grinned. "Well, if anyone can do it, it's you, Emma. You worked twice as hard for half the pay as the rest of the nursing student intern friends to earn your first job on the swing shift in the ER. Once you have a goal in mind, Emma, you don't stop until you achieve it."

"Never."

The two women exchanged a glance. Emma was dogged, true. She'd had to be. Raising her younger sister alone since the age of eighteen made her that way. Her strength had come at a price. Profound loss.

Besides, she'd worked far too hard for far too long to get where she was now and no way would one entitled, cranky hermit of a surgeon knock her off her game. "So, does that mean I can head upstairs to wait for Dr. Markson?"

Dr. Franklin and Jane looked at each other, then back to Emma. Dr. Franklin gave a curt nod. "Go. But don't say I didn't warn you. We'll see you at the press conference in half an hour."

Eight hours earlier

Dr. Thaddeus Markson scowled up at the speaker in the elevator where incessant singers went on and on about halls and holly and fa-la-la-la-la—whatever the hell that meant— then jammed the button for his floor again, like that would make the thing move faster.

Christmas was nothing but an excuse to overspend, overindulge and generally overcompensate for all the other days of the year when you were grossly underwhelming. He hated it, more than any other day of the year. Thad would much rather be spectacular in the other 364 calendar boxes and ignore the twenty-fifth and all its overblown pageantry entirely. Which hopefully he'd be able to do just fine because he planned to work all that day, as usual.

Speaking of work, he was here at Manhattan West to perform a delicate surgery only he could do. As the city's top cardiothoracic surgeon, he was used to getting called in when lives were on the line.

Finally, the bell dinged and the doors swished open and Thad stepped out onto the surgical floor.

"What have we got?" he asked Dr. Imrani, the surgeon who'd met him there and now walked with him to the staff locker room. The Iranian man had recently moved to Manhattan from the UK specifically to be part of the innovative cardiovascular team at Manhattan West. "We're sure it's an aortic dissection?" Aortic dissections were rare and involved a tear in the inner layer of the body's main artery, the aorta. Without surgical intervention, the artery could rupture completely, and the patient would bleed to death internally. It was a long, delicate procedure that required steady hands and impeccable skills, both of which Thad possessed in abundance.

"Yes." Dr. Imrani kept pace with Thad as they headed through a set of automatic double doors, and he gave Thad the rundown from the other side of the lockers while Thad changed out of his tailor-made suit and tugged on standard-issue blue cotton scrubs instead. "Patient is a sixty-one-year-old previously healthy male who presented to the emergency department complaining of chest discomfort and shortness of breath."

Once he'd changed, Thad checked the app on his phone that monitored his blood sugar through a sensor Thad wore on his skin and was connected to the insulin pump he wore for long surgeries such as this one, which could last up to eight hours. As a type 1 diabetic, he'd spent years making sure his condition in no way impeded his abilities as a surgeon, and today was no different. He'd eaten right before he'd gotten called in for this procedure, so he should be good to go for a while.

"Any history of blunt force trauma?" Thad asked as he put his phone away, then closed the locker and joined the other doctor to go into a room with a long metal sink against one wall. He stepped on the lever bar below to start the water and washed his hands and forearms with surgical-grade antibacterial soap and hot water. "Car accident?"

"No." The trauma surgeon chuckled. "Believe it or not, the patient was skiing and got hit in the chest by a snowboarder on the side of a mountain." At Thad's blank look, he fidgeted. "'Tis the season and all."

He grunted, scowling as he started soaping up his left hand and lower arm. Another reason to dislike the holiday, apparently. Death by disaster. "What else?"

The trauma surgeon continued. "After the injury, patient got up without incident, developing pain along the left sternum about thirty minutes later, which he said quickly resolved. He then drove the approximate two to three hours home. Patient stated later that afternoon, he complained to his wife of a 'hollow sensation' in his chest that worsened with deep inhalation, and some mild shortness of breath with exertion. He presented this afternoon at the urging of his wife. On initial evaluation, he denied any nausea, vomiting, diaphoresis, back pain or fever, and was comfortable at rest. No neurologic complaints. He did note a contusion of his left lower leg from a fall on ice one week prior. No past medical history, no medications, nonsmoker, exercises regularly, and no family history of cardiac or connective tissue disease." The other doctor scrolled through more notes on his tablet as Thad finished washing. "In triage, blood pressure was one hundred over eighty, pulse seventy, respiratory rate twenty.

O-stats one hundred percent on room air, and temp ninety-nine point seven. Heart sounds normal on exam with no murmurs, lungs clear bilaterally, and no tenderness to palpation of the sternum or ribs or external signs of trauma. Abdomen non-tender. A small hematoma noted on the left calf. Neurologic examination grossly normal."

Thad lifted his foot to shut off the water in the sink, then shook off the excess moisture from his hands. "And the EKG?"

"Normal sinus rhythm with minimal non-specific T-wave abnormalities. No evidence of pneumothorax, pulmonary contusion, rib fractures or widened mediastinum on chest X-ray."

Thad gave a curt nod. Chest X-rays were not reliable in diagnosing aortic trauma. "And what did the CTA show?"

"Bovine-type aortic arch with both carotid arteries arising from the brachiocephalic artery, and a type-A aortic dissection extending from the aortic root to beyond the bilateral renal arteries." Which basically just meant two arteries shared the same starting point, like two branches off the same trunk, versus two separate trees. Not uncommon really, especially with patients of African descent, as was the current patient. The tear in the artery had occurred right at the point where the kidneys received their blood supply. Not good at all.

He backed out yet another door, arms held up in front of him, into the operating theater. A surgical tech suited him in a sterile gown, gloves and mask before Thad moved to the table where their patient was already under anesthesia and prepped for him to start.

Long procedures like this one took a team to complete, and Thad glanced at the men and women around the table as he took a scalpel from the surgical nurse. Because of the location of the injury, they would first need to perform an open bypass on the patient to ensure that Thad had a bloodless field in which to graft the damaged aorta. The surgical team included not only Thad but a second cardiac surgeon, interventional cardiologists, a thoracic surgeon, and vascular and interventional radiologists. All of them had roles to play as the procedure progressed.

With a curt nod, Thad stepped forward. "Let's get started."

Five hours in, he'd finally sewn a Dacron aortic graft into place on the man's aorta and was currently reattaching the important blood vessels to it as the patient's heart beat against the back of Thad's right hand where it was held in a sling, safely out of the way. The patient had also been placed into hypothermic circulatory arrest, which was a fancy way of saying they'd lowered the man's body temperature to slow the cellular activity and allow them to stop the blood flow temporarily, as needed. The constant low white noise of the heart-lung bypass machine keeping the patient alive helped Thad stay focused and alert as he raced against the clock.

He'd yet to lose a patient and wasn't about to start now.

By the time they finally closed the patient up, the man's heart was beating on its own again and his lungs worked fine. They'd keep him under general anesthesia for another four to six hours, then move him to the ICU for a day or two. If there were no complications, he'd spend seven to ten days at Manhattan West before going home.

Thad scrubbed down again, then returned to the locker room to change. It had been a long night, and a glance at his Omega watch showed it was well into the morning hours now. All he wanted was a hot shower and a long sleep. But what he found, waiting in front of his locker, was a smiling woman wearing a bright green sweater with a reindeer on the front, looking like she'd stepped off the front of a greeting card. For a second, Thad wondered if he'd slipped into some kind of glycemic hallucination without knowing it.

"Dr. Markson," she said, cheerful as one of Santa's elves, setting Thad's teeth on edge. She seemed vaguely familiar to him, but he couldn't place from where and didn't want to bother at that point. It had been a grueling day and he just wanted to go home.

"How did you get in here?" he said, moving past her to his locker. "Only hospital staff are allowed in this area. I could have you arrested for trespassing."

Seemingly undeterred by his churlishness, she continued to smile. "I work here, Dr. Markson. Emma Trudeau." She held out a hand to him, which he promptly ignored. "I'm a nurse in the emergency department here at Manhattan West. We've worked a couple of cases together in the ER."

Well, that explained the familiarity then. Thad turned away to begin pulling out his clothes. "What do you want?"

Most people, when confronted with his brusque manner, either scurried away or simply gave up. It both impressed and irritated him that this petite woman did neither. He did not have the time or patience for this tonight. Normally, Thad would never disrobe in front of a stranger, but given she seemed to have no qualms about invading his personal boundaries, he gave little regard to hers and pulled off his scrub shirt, leaving him bare-chested.

"I…" She stopped when his shirt came off, her bright smile fading a little as her cheeks heated. Then she looked away fast and cleared her throat, her perky tone back in place. "I've been put in charge of the hospital's holiday charity event this year, our Wish Star Program."

"My condolences."

His sarcasm bounced off her like sunlight off an icicle and she continued unfazed. "As part of my preplanning I was tasked with finding a partner to help me with the event. Someone whose qualities would complement my own and help to make this year's Wish Star Program the best one ever."

Thad paused in the middle of buttoning his dress shirt to stare at her, one brow raised. He didn't like where this was headed one bit. "And that has anything to do with me how?"

"I've chosen you to be my partner." She beamed at him like that was some kind of honor. In other circumstances, Thad might have found her attractive, might have said her smile was nice. Very nice. Now it was one more nuisance he didn't need.

"No." He undid the tie at the waist of his scrub pants. "And unless you'd like a full strip show, I suggest you turn around."

Her wide dark eyes flickered down to his lower half then back up before she swiftly pivoted away, her cheeks pink again. Thad couldn't say the last time he'd met a woman who blushed. Would've been endearing if this whole situation wasn't so annoying. The pump at his lower back beeped a notification, signaling he needed to eat soon. He quickly pulled on his suit pants and tucked in his shirt before zipping up and buckling his Italian leather belt. He did not have time for this nonsense.

"No?" she asked, the word emerging as more of a squeak from where she faced away from him.

"No," Thad repeated as he sat down to put on his shoes. With her turned away, he had a chance to assess her. Slim, with a slight curviness to her hips and behind. Long dark hair, braided neatly, hanging down her back. For a second he wondered if those braids felt as soft as they looked before he shoved that silliness aside. He was exhausted and hungry, that's all. "I have neither the time nor the interest to participate in your little project, Nurse…"

"Trudeau," she said, a tad firmer this time. "Emma Trudeau."

Thad took a deep breath, then tugged on his suit coat and grabbed his phone before closing his locker and tossing his dirty scrubs into a biohazard laundry bin nearby before heading for the exit. She probably wanted money. That seemed to be the most common "quality" people saw in him. "I'll write you a check. How much?"

"Excuse me?" she said, following him.

"If it's over a hundred thousand, it will take longer because I'll have to go through my accountants to liquidate some assets." Thad walked out into the brightly lit hall and toward the elevators, not slowing down for her at all. "If it's under that amount, I'll have someone drop off a check tomorrow. Who should I make it out to? The hospital or the charity?"

"I don't want your money, Dr. Markson," Nurse Trudeau said, waiting with him at the elevators. She was harder to shake than a two-ton snow globe. Her voice held an edge of steel now, her posture stiffer. "I want your help with this project. The planning, the preparing, the execution."

Thad sighed, staring at the metal doors in front of him. "And I've told you what I can do."

"No, you haven't." She stepped a little closer, invading his personal space, a hint of her spicy-sweet scent surrounding him. "Dr. Markson, I realize this might be a foreign concept to a man such as yourself, but sometimes actual physical participation is a good thing."

Thad scowled. "Physical participation?"

"Being present. Being involved. That's what I mean. Getting your hands dirty."

The elevator dinged and Thad hurried onboard, hoping to get away from his new, bothersome shadow, but no such luck. The woman followed him onto the elevator, then shut the doors on them, effectively locking him inside with her. "I need your help. I've already discussed it with the HR director and the chief of staff in a meeting earlier and they agree it would be good for you to participate. You have connections within the city to get this done quickly, and that's what I need. The wish is due on Christmas Eve, so only a month away. That's not long to help a child in need."

Again with Christmas. Why was it haunting him this year? He stared at his reflection in the mirrored wall of the compartment across from him. Connections. She wanted his connections. Of course she did. Thad had learned from a young age that wealth meant power, and power brought out the worst in people. Everyone wanted something from him, even if it was just to disappear off the face of the earth, like his own father had. Well, Thad was through granting favors.

"A check. That's the extent of my offer to you, Nurse Trudeau. Take it or leave it. I have time for nothing else."

They arrived at the lobby and the doors opened. Thad walked out with Nurse Trudeau on his heels and headed toward the side exit, past the atrium. As he passed the Christmas tree, he found himself herded toward a small crowd gathered there, with lights blazing and cameras whirring.

"What the—?" He tried to pull free of Nurse Trudeau's grip on his arm but found her harder to evade than he'd first guessed. "Unhand me!"

She let him go then, her smile back in place as they faced Dr. John Franklin and Jane Ayashi from HR.

"I'd like to file a formal complaint against this woman." He pointed at Nurse Trudeau. "She's been accosting me since I left the OR about some charity thing I want nothing to do with."

"Later," John said, nudging Thad to turn around and face the crowd. A lectern had been set up in front of them. "After the press conference."

"Press conference?" Thad's voice grew louder than the blood pounding in his ears. He felt out of control at that moment and hated it. "I'm not doing any press conference. I've not agreed to anything. My time is too valuable to waste on toy shopping or pizza parties." He glared over at Nurse Trudeau, who now stood shoulder to shoulder with him as they formed a line behind the lectern. "And you can forget about the check now, too."

"Never wanted it in the first place," she shot back, her gaze straight ahead, her smile firm. "Help, Dr. Markson. You're going to help me, and help a sick child, whether you like it or not. It'll be good for you."

"How dare you—" Thad blustered, only to be cut off by Dr. Franklin stepping up to the lectern.

"Thank you all for coming," Dr. Franklin said, his deep voice echoing through the atrium like a herald of angels on high. "Our two Manhattan representatives, Nurse

Emma Trudeau and Dr. Thaddeus Markson, are partnering this year to make one lucky child's holiday wish come true on behalf of Manhattan West General Hospital. Nurse Trudeau, if you'd like to select a wish star…"

All eyes turned to the woman beside Thad, and she swallowed hard. Was she suddenly nervous? Good. Thad hoped she was after putting him through all this. He lived like a hermit for a reason and that was to avoid situations exactly like this one. How dare she impose herself like this on him? Who did she think she was?

He watched as she stepped up to the massive tree in the atrium. The thing had to be at least thirty feet high to reach the top. And the lower third was covered with stars handmade by kids in the Pediatric Intensive Care Unit here at Manhattan West. All colors and sizes and shapes of wrapping paper and glitter-covered cardboard. Thad's chest constricted even more, this time from painful memories of creating a star like this himself when he'd been little. Not that he'd needed charity, but his caregivers had insisted he make one anyway…

In an instant he was back in that cold, lonely hospital room, staring out the window at the snow falling and wishing he was anywhere else but there…

Applause broke out as Nurse Trudeau selected a star, jarring Thad back to the present.

She walked over to Dr. Franklin at the lectern.

"Which child's is it?" one of the reporters asked. "What did they wish for?"

Nurse Trudeau stepped up to the microphone. "This year's Wish Star recipient is Ricky Lynch," she said. "He's nine and he's got a brain tumor." She blinked down at the star in her hands. From where Thad stood he could see the painstakingly neatly printed bold block letters "He wants a carnival, with free candy and games and a carousel, for all the kids in the Manhattan West Pediatric Intensive Care Unit to ride."

The words slowly penetrated the fog of adrenaline in Thad's brain. *Oh God. A carnival?*

He'd wished for something similar on his star all those years ago. A tiny pinch pricked from the center of Thad's chest, somewhere in the vicinity of his heart.

No. No, no, no.

He refused to allow his past to rule over him again. He'd spent far too long locking it away where it belonged. And certainly not for some woman who'd bamboozled him into this whole situation in the first place.

Not happening.

Cameras clicked and reporters shouted more questions at them, but Thad didn't care about any of it. He only cared about getting out of there and away from all of this horrible mess and even more so away from the woman who was now standing beside him again, smiling and holding his arm like he was a willing participant in all this. Worst of all, it felt nice, her touching him. Oddly comforting. As if he wasn't alone anymore, as he'd been alone so long. And that's when he knew he needed to leave. Now.

With more force than was probably necessary, Thad yanked free and walked away from the crowd, ignoring the calls of his name behind him. All he wanted was to get back to the safety of his town house, get away from these people, get locked away in his study and never come out again. He was Thad Markson, of the New York Marksons, and he did not have time to deal with organizing a charity event or making a kid's wish come true or the most annoyingly attractive woman he'd met in years. Maybe ever.

"Dr. Markson," Nurse Trudeau called after him, but he was already out the door.

Bah humbug indeed.

CHAPTER TWO

THE SUBWAY RIDE from the apartment she shared with her sister in Richmond Hill, Queens, to the Upper East Side of Manhattan was a nightmare, as usual, this time of year. The guy next to Emma had fallen asleep, then snored and drooled all over her shoulder for nearly the entire way. Emma had ignored him as best she could, concentrating on her Kindle instead.

Her phone pinged as soon as she stepped off the train and onto the platform at the Fifty-Ninth Street station. Maybe it was Dr. Markson returning her call at last. She'd been trying to contact him since the night of the wish star drawing with no luck. Now it had been a week with no response from him. Thanksgiving had been and gone, and time was marching on. She'd worked the holiday, of course, to make up for short staffing in the ER. She and Karley had celebrated afterward in their apartment, with turkey subs from down the street and playing video games together.

But unfortunately, as she scowled down at her phone, it wasn't a message from Dr. Markson. Just another reminder her automatic payment for her school loans was due next week.

Great.

With a sigh, she shoved the phone back in her pocket, tightened her scarf around her neck against the brisk wind and started for Dr. Markson's town house on the corner of Sixty-Third Street and Fifth Avenue, right across from Central Park. Couldn't get an address any posher in New York. The man obviously wanted nothing to do with her or the project, but Emma was undeterred.

If the Grinch wouldn't come to her, she'd go to the Grinch.

As she made her way up Fifth Avenue, Emma smiled behind her scarf at the shops full of Christmas decorations and the stone and vintage facades of the buildings lining the street adorned in red and green lights for the season. Gorgeous. No one did Christmas like her beloved hometown of NYC.

A short time later she stopped and stared up at a four-story building. Red brick on the top two floors, gray stone on the bottom two. Plus, a basement, if the black door to the left of the front stoop was any indication. The place was probably worth more than Emma would make in her entire life. She wondered if it had been passed down in Dr. Markson's family, like many of the places along here. Most of these townhomes had been built back during the Gilded Age of the 1910s by the newly wealthy industrial barons of the time. Emma was something of a history buff, too.

She shook off those errant thoughts. Didn't matter when or how Dr. Markson had gotten his fancy house. All that mattered was him doing his part to make this holiday carnival happen.

Emma took a deep breath, then climbed the granite stoop to the front door before knocking the heavy gilded lion head against the black painted wood door. Soon, an intercom on the wall beside her crackled to life.

"Yes?" said a snooty man's voice. Not Dr. Markson. Emma would remember his voice anywhere, after hearing him giving one of the residents in the ER hell one day for talking over Dr. Markson in front of a patient. The fact that the information the resident had given was probably incomplete didn't help either, but still.

"I'm here to see Dr. Markson, please?" Emma pulled her scarf away from her face for the camera and cleared her throat. "Thank you."

Several seconds ticked by before the man responded "I'm sorry, but you aren't on the roster. If you have a delivery, the service entrance is in the back alley."

"No delivery. Dr. Markson and I are working on a special project for Manhattan West General. My name is Emma Trudeau and I'm a nurse at the hospital. I must speak with him. It's an emergency."

Okay, maybe the last part was a stretch, but time was ticking.

More time passed. So much so Emma feared he'd stopped answering the intercom entirely. Then, finally, a lock clicked and the door opened to reveal an older man, maybe late seventies, dressed in a gray butler's uniform. Huh. Emma thought those only existed in movies.

The man's chilly stare rivaled the subzero temperatures outside, his expression emotionless. "You may wait in the foyer while I speak with Dr. Markson."

Considering her booted toes were already

numb, Emma took the man up on his offer, stepping inside to gape at her surroundings while the older man disappeared up the carved wooden staircase to her right.

From what she could see from where she stood, the gorgeous first floor had once been an old-fashioned parlor, with lots of creamy marble and warm cherrywood trim. Large windows filled the opposite wall across from her and revealed a large garden area in the back of the town house, complete with sculptures and stone benches. While dormant now, Emma bet it was beautiful in the spring.

Emma leaned slightly to peer through the doorway to her right and saw a sitting room bigger than her entire apartment. Light yellow walls, same inlaid marble floors and a huge TV over an elegant carved fireplace that took up practically one entire wall. In front of it were a pair of sprawling cream-colored sofas. If she leaned to her left, she caught a glimpse of what looked like a formal dining room, with a large dining table surrounded by twelve chairs, like something out of Buckingham Palace. Emma tried to imagine the prickly Dr. Markson she knew from the ER living here and had a hard time picturing the stiff, stuffy man ever relaxing anywhere. Then again, the place was pristine, more like a museum than a house, so maybe he only slept and changed in this place.

Emma chuckled and tucked her mittens in her pocket. The rich were a whole different beast. One she hoped to tame to help her with the project, no matter how long it took.

"Sir, there's someone downstairs to see you," his butler said from the door of the third-floor study.

Thad looked up from his computer and scowled. He hated being interrupted during work. "Who is it? No. I don't care. Get rid of them."

Everett, Thad's assistant, valet and now close friend, never changed his stoic expression. Growing up, the older man's stoicism used to annoy Thad, but now he welcomed it.

The butler had been with the Markson family for as long as Thad could remember. Trained in all aspects of running a household to discreet perfection, Everett's skills were legendary and sought-after in wealthy circles. In his seventies now, the man retained a distinguished full head of white hair, a mustache and a penchant for wearing expensive suits when off duty. He brought a solid presence and capability Thad found soothing. In many ways, the man was more of a father to him than his own had ever been.

And truthfully, he needed Everett. Having the butler around kept Thad from almost complete isolation between his surgical consultations. He wasn't antisocial really; he just had his reasons for valuing his privacy.

A whimper issued near Thad's feet and Thad dropped his hand to pet the black Lab laying there. "What's the matter, Baxter? Huh, boy?"

The dog's wet nose pressed against his palm and Thad smiled. Between his dog and his butler, he had plenty of company. No need to be lonely at all. Never mind the pinch near his heart. It was fine. He was fine. More than enough of everything to last a lifetime.

"I tried to tell her you weren't available, sir. Many times." Annoyance edged Everett's tone. "She said you're working on a project together at the hospital and that it was an emergency. Since the weather is bitterly cold today, I let her wait in the foyer."

Dammit. He'd thought he'd escaped the whole wish mess with that charity event the other night. He'd offered money and it was all he was prepared to give. "Tell her I've left. And to find someone else to help with her project. I'm not available." If she wouldn't take his money, there was nothing more he could offer. Thad had no time to spare with his difficult surgery coming up next month. There were new procedures to study, cutting-edge theories and practices to memorize.

A lifetime of pain and regrets to keep buried.

Thad shook the last thought off. He rarely thought of his childhood these days, how he'd had to scramble for scraps of affection from his father as a child. The grief that had taken over his entire life after the horrible accident that had taken Thad's mother away when he'd been only ten.

He squeezed the pencil in his hand so tightly it broke.

Everett cleared his throat. "Would you like me to throw her out, sir?"

Ah, hell. Thad inhaled deeply, dropping the pencil shards on his desk, then glaring down at the medical journal article he'd been reading on his laptop. He did not have time for this. Any of this. Distractions were rarely a problem for him, not with his usual laser-type focus, but this whole situation had him flustered.

Baxter cocked his head again at Thad, his inky black fur gleaming in the flickering light from the fireplace. He dusted his

hands off, his fingers shaking slightly, a sign
his blood sugar was dropping. And yes, perhaps he had ignored the alerts from his sensor and pump because he was immersed in
studying. He'd eat, later, when it was con-
venient. His kitchen was well stocked with
items to fend off a hypoglycemic storm, if
needed. Juices and candy and even special
fast-acting glucose gels to dissolve under his
tongue. Everett knew where to find them all
quickly. He'd become something of a nurse
as well over the years, on top of his other duties. Thad wasn't sure what he'd do when the
older man retired.

Forcing his mind away from such a mel-
ancholy thought, Thad focused on Baxter
again, who was licking Thad's hand again.
If only the dog wasn't such a big softy, he'd
send him down to scare the woman away.
Unfortunately, Baxter was more likely to
welcome her with a lolling tongue and wagging tail.

Thad tapped a few keys on his laptop and
brought up the feeds from the town house's
numerous security cameras, scrolling through
them until a grainy black-and-white image
of a young Black woman dressed in a silly
hat and scarf standing in his foyer appeared.
She bounced on the balls of her feet, hands

in her coat pockets, leaning around to see into the rooms on the first floor. His shoulders sagged. Why couldn't she take the hint? He wasn't going to meet with her. Not today. Not ever. "Let her wait. Eventually, she'll get tired or bored, and leave."

His butler nodded, but the older man's gaze held a hint of doubt. "As you wish, sir."

Good. Done. Thad never second-guessed himself. A quality that made him a great surgeon. He returned to reading his article. Once that was done, he logged into a special website to watch the video of the surgery being performed, committing each step of the delicate operation to his memory. Closed his eyes and imagined himself working on the patient, going step-by-step to repair the damage to their cardiovascular system. He'd studied this particular procedure for close to a year now, making minor tweaks as needed to meet his patient's specific situation, going through each step over and over, in preparation.

Next month, he would finally perform it to save a woman's life.

Doing the procedure itself and having a successful outcome were accolades enough for him. He wasn't charging the patient or her family at all for his services. They didn't have much, so Thad had also arranged to pay for the hospital and any other expenses associated with the surgery—including the patient's travel from Central America—through the private foundation he'd set up via his attorneys years ago. Everything totally anonymous. A way to give back without the world knowing his business. Another way to rinse away the stain of his family's sins. He couldn't save the world, but he could give his patients a new, healthier future.

Time passed in a blur as Thad absorbed the detailed images playing on his screen, until finally, he sat back, neck stiff and spine cracking. "All done, Baxter."

The Lab yawned.

"Now, let's go eat, huh?" Thad stood from behind his desk and stretched.

They walked downstairs from his office on the third-floor to the second-floor kitchen, Thad's balance a bit wobbly. The pump at his waist, tucked into his pants, again beeped ominously. Damn. He just needed a quick hit of sugar to stabilize things. It would be fine. Yes, as a doctor, he should know better than to let things get out of hand like this, but he'd been working. And his work was everything to him. He stepped into the massive chef's kitchen, Baxter whimpering and nudging his leg, and opened the fridge for a bottle of apple juice, glancing at the flat-screen monitor on the wall and freezing.

Son of a...

The digital clock above his Viking range showed nearly two hours had passed since he'd told Everett to let the woman wait, figuring she'd leave eventually. But no. There she was. Still standing in his foyer, stubbornly facing his camera now. Even with the grainy footage, her loveliness made his heart skip a beat. Dark eyes surrounded by lush lashes. Full lips slightly parted as if waiting for a kiss. Still bouncing on the balls of her feet, too, like her body could barely contain all the energy inside it. An unwanted tingle of awareness warmed Thad's belly, spreading quickly outward before he quashed it.

No. This was not happening. He refused to be attracted to this woman.

Frustration coursed through him. Why couldn't the world let him be? Outside the windows, snow fell heavier and the wind howled. A storm was coming, in more ways than one.

Pissed, he set his bottle of juice aside, unopened. She wanted to see him? Fine. Thad would make sure she never forgot the experience. His hands were trembling so bad now he gripped the edge of the counter to keep his balance.

Everett stood in the doorway leading to the stairs. "Sir, do you need—"

"Show her up," Thad growled, aware that at least some of his anger was due to his lowering blood sugar, but beyond caring at this point.

"Sir, I—a…" Everett started toward him, his expression concerned.

"No!" Thad shouted, then lowered his voice, the trembling worse. "Get her up here now. I want this over with, once and for all."

The butler stared at him a moment, then hurried down the stairs. "Yes, sir."

Baxter nudged Thad's leg with his nose, whimpering louder, and everything went sideways.

"Follow me," Everett said, turning toward those stairs again, moving faster now. "Hurry."

The urgency in the older man's voice surprised her, but Emma wasn't about to lose her chance to see Dr. Markson. Not after she'd waited forever and a day here. She shook out her stiff legs and followed the butler, scared to touch anything for fear she'd leave a mark on the gleaming wood. They'd made it halfway up a second flight of stairs when a shattering of glass split the air.

"Hurry, ma'am," the butler said again, showing admirable agility for his age.

Emma's pulse stumbled as they raced up the rest of the stairs. "What's going on?"

They entered an enormous kitchen, which should have been a showpiece, too, but instead was in complete disarray. Cabinet doors open and food scattered everywhere across the countertops. In the open doors of a huge, professional-sized double-sided refrigerator, Dr. Markson stood with his back to them, rummaging inside, a shattered crystal tumbler and a cowering dog at his feet. He didn't seem to notice them or the mess.

Everett immediately ran to a drawer and pulled out a pack of glucose gels. "He's a type 1 diabetic, ma'am. He doesn't always take care of himself as he should."

"Right." Emma moved into action. Carefully kicking the broken glass out of the way with her boot, before placing a hand on Dr. Markson's back and noticing the bulge of an insulin pump at his waist. "Why don't you have a seat, Dr. Markson, and Everett will help you feel better."

He spun around, blue eyes wild and glassy and face gaunt. Classic signs of hypoglycemia. Neglecting himself was one thing, but letting your blood sugar drop to dangerously low levels could be life-threatening.

"Don't touch me. Leave me alone!" Dr. Markson growled, turning back to the counter to scatter more food around. A banana flew past her head, then a jar of jam, which broke into a sticky mess on the gray marble floor behind her.

The dog gave a startled yelp and Emma reached down to give the poor thing a pat, noticing the collar embroidered with Service Dog in white. "It's okay, sweetie. We're here now and we'll take care of him."

"Don't need care," Dr. Markson hissed, pushing Emma out of the way hard with his hip, causing her to stumble back a little and barely miss stepping on the dog's paw. "Don't need anyone."

"We could use those glucose gels over here," she called to the butler. "And juice. Something to get in his system fast."

Everett handed her the package of gels, then grabbed the apple juice Thad had pulled from the fridge earlier. "Ready when you are, ma'am."

"Okay. Good." Emma switched into ER nurse mode then, her tone brisk and efficient.

"Help me get him to one of those stools at the island and sit him down."

While Everett steered Dr. Markson away from the fridge, Emma got the juice bottle open while keeping the dog back with her foot. The butler got her patient onto the stool, and Emma crouched in front of Dr. Markson, smiling. "Hello, there. Remember me? Emma Trudeau, a nurse from the hospital. Can you take a sip of this juice for me, please?"

She held the bottle to his lips, but he batted it away. "No! I don't want your drink. I don't want you here! Leave me alone!" Emma's heart sank a bit at his cruel tone, but she held her ground. Aggression was a common side effect of low blood sugar. This wasn't him. Not really. He needed some sugar in his system. Easier said than done, though, given that Dr. Markson had more muscle on him than she'd previously noticed. Still, she persisted. "Come on. Please. Just a little drink."

His eyes were more unfocused, as if the world around him made no sense. Screw it. Time for the gels. Emma normally used them as a last resort in the ER, since they were pure sugar and could easily send a patient in the opposite problem if not carefully monitored, but desperate times called for desperate measures. She ripped the top of a sachet and prepared to squeeze the contents into Thad's mouth. "Hold his head for me."

The older man did as she asked, his face tight with worry, and Emma squeezed the gel into his mouth. She'd guessed on the dosage based on his size, but they'd deal with the consequences afterward. She held his mouth closed until he swallowed.

Slowly, Thad began to quiet. Five minutes passed and she was able to get him to drink some juice, too. Part of her itched to check his sensor to see his levels, but she didn't want to disturb him again until he was stable.

"Will he be all right, ma'am?" Everett asked, a bit of his color returning. "He hasn't been this bad in a long time."

Emma straightened and leaned her hip against the edge of the giant granite-topped island. "He should be all right. We'll need to wait and see."

CHAPTER THREE

AN ANGEL FLOATED before him. An angel with long black braids and bright dark eyes. She also had a pink hat on her head with a ball on top that flopped around whenever she moved. Weird. His dreams didn't normally look like this.

The angel patted his hand and talked quietly to him, her voice calm and soothing. The voice he'd wished for as a child on those long nights after his mother had died and his father had grown cold and distant. The voice of reason and truth and kindness. He smiled.

"Sir?" Another voice interrupted his fantasy, dissolving the cloudy, comfortable heaven in his head. Thad moved and winced, his back aching. And cold. He was so cold. A shudder ran through him as he straightened, doing his best to shake off the fuzziness surrounding him. "Are you feeling better?"

Everett. Yep, he recognized that voice.

What he didn't recognize was the edge of fear in the butler's voice. Thad could be a bit brusque and broody sometimes, but Everett had never been scared of him. Probably because the man had seen Thad in diapers. Hard to fear a man you'd seen in his undies.

A cold nose nudged the strip of bare leg between the top of Thad's sock and the hem of his pants. Baxter. He absently reached down to pat the Lab's head to reassure him. Good old Baxter. His father had never let Thad have pets in the town house, so the first thing he'd done after his father died five years ago had been to rescue Baxter. The dog had returned the favor many times over.

Thad's mystery angel still hovered around the periphery of his vision, though, speaking again. "Hi, Dr. Markson. Glad you're back with us." She didn't wait for his answer. Just as well, with his thick, dry mouth. He licked his lips and tasted apple. Huh. He didn't remember drinking juice.

He sat there until his brain functioned again and tiny puzzle pieces fell into place—working upstairs; pushing himself too hard for too long; the trip to the kitchen for food.

His angel touched his arm and all Thad's senses sparked to life. Normally, he didn't like people touching him. So invasive. Left him feeling unsettled and vulnerable. Thad hated being vulnerable.

Frowning, he shrugged off her touch and blinked hard to clear his vision. Turned to look at her, his movements slow and awkward. "Who are you?"

The woman smiled, her teeth white and even against her darker skin, and held out her hand. "Emma Trudeau. We've met before. I'm a nurse in the ER at Manhattan West and your new partner for the hospital's holiday wish project."

Thad shifted his attention to his butler, who stood near the fridge now with Baxter, a broom in one hand. "Everett, what's happening here?"

His words sounded funny to his own ears. Slurred as if he'd been drinking, but Thad never touched alcohol. Dulled the senses and affected the reflexes. As he took in the chaotic mess in his kitchen, Thad's scowl deepened. He did stand then, his wobbly knees accepting his weight thankfully, though he still held on to the island just in case. "Will someone please explain what the hell happened in here?"

The last thing Thad remembered was getting into the fridge. He ran a shaky hand down the front of his black cashmere turtleneck, before giving Emma Trudeau some serious side-eye. She'd helped him…apparently, and he wasn't sure how he felt about that. Thad didn't like surprises. Or changes.

Tonight, he'd had both.

His stomach plummeted as the realization of what had happened struck him hard. Oh God. He hadn't let things slip that badly with his blood sugar since way back in his teens, after he'd first been diagnosed with type 1 diabetes at twelve. At the time he'd first found out about his disease, his life had been in turmoil anyway. His beloved mother had died unexpectedly two years prior, and his father had not handled it well. He'd thrown himself into work, leaving young Thad to deal with his grief on his own. Then, after Thad had gotten sick and been hospitalized because of his blood sugar and received his final diagnosis, Thad's father had basically shunned him. Said he was deficient, weak, useless, because of his illness. Part of Thad's drive to not just succeed but excel came from the deep hurt of his father's rejection back then. His father had died five years ago, but those wounds lived on, festering inside where Thad had buried them because it was easier that way. He was fine. It was fine.

Or he had been, until now.

Dammit. Why hadn't he taken two seconds to check his blood sugar earlier like he'd intended? He certainly knew the drill by now, the symptoms to look out for that meant he was headed for trouble. He even kept snacks all around the town house just for such emergencies.

Shame heated his cheeks as his father's voice echoed through his head from the past.

Deficient, weak. Useless.

"Dr. Markson?" the nurse asked again. She tapped his arm to get his attention. Her smile had been replaced by a serious expression now. "Where is your glucose monitor? We should check your levels now after what just happened."

He knew that. Of course he did. But having her tell him, like he was a child, only made him angry. Rather than answer her, Thad walked to the sink instead, broken glass crunching under his shoes. He scowled down at them. "Who broke this?"

Thad hated disorder. That was another reason he preferred to live alone. No one around to make a mess.

Everett rushed over with a broom and dustpan from the closet nearby to begin sweeping up the shards. "I wasn't here to see it happen, but we believe you did, sir."

"We?" Thad's exasperation reached a breaking point. What the hell was happening in his own house? And since when did Everett join forces with anyone against him? They'd known each other for decades. Then a nurse shows up and suddenly they're a team? No. He didn't like that at all.

The older man threw the broken glass in the trash then turned back to Thad. "Yes, sir. I brought Ms. Trudeau up here as you'd asked and when we arrived, we found you going through the cupboards and refrigerator. We weren't quite sure what you were doing."

The final missing piece of the puzzle fell into place for Thad with a heavy thud in his head, his humiliation complete. "I did this."

It wasn't a question.

Emma stepped in beside him. "Is there somewhere we can talk, Dr. Markson?"

"No, Ms. Trudeau," Thad gritted out, his inner discombobulation and embarrassment at having lost control like that erupting into anger. "There isn't. We have nothing to talk about. I will not be participating in any project with you, and I want you to leave my home right now. I want you to leave me alone, period. Understand?"

Usually when Thad lost his temper, people jumped. Not Emma Trudeau, though. Nope.

In fact, she didn't look surprised or fazed at all. The woman stood her ground, crossing her arms like she had no intention of going anywhere. "What I understand, Dr. Markson," she said, "is that we're both busy people and I for one don't have time to deal with this nonsense. We—" she gestured between them "—have an important project to complete in order to make a very sick child's holiday wish come true. In addition to that, I have way too much riding on getting this thing done that I won't allow you or anyone else to stand in my way. Do you understand?"

He blinked at her, too stunned to respond. No one talked back to him like that. Ever.

"Now," she said, leaning forward slightly, enough for him to catch a whiff of her rose-and-cinnamon scent. "We are going to talk. Here or somewhere else in this palace, that's up to you. But it's happening."

When had the kitchen gotten so hot? Emma took off her coat, hat and scarf and handed them over to Everett, who waited to take them, seemingly as anxious to escape the tension in the room as the black Lab took up residence at Dr. Markson's side once more, lying down on the tile floor. Good service dog and not uncommon for people who had chronic conditions like Dr. Markson's. Her face burned hotter than the sun and Emma desperately wanted to fan herself but doubted it would help. Not with Dr. Markson watching her from such close quarters. Something about the man seemed to set all her senses abuzz. Even with the icy glare he currently directed her way.

Working with him, even temporarily, would be a baptism by fire, no doubt. But Emma had never been one to run from a challenge and she refused to start now. The clock above his fancy stove said it was nearly eight o'clock, meaning she'd been waiting to see this man for hours. Hours she could've spent at home with her sister, Karley, relaxing. Maybe catching up on the latest episodes of the new rom-com that had dropped earlier in the week on streaming. Emma had precious little free time to begin with and it seemed Dr. Markson would be eating into what small amount she had left. At least for the next three weeks or so.

She gestured toward the pump at his waist, then the sensor on his arm, hidden beneath the sleeve of his soft-looking black turtleneck sweater. "Looks like you've got the latest equipment, so I'm guessing your blood sugar is monitored through an app on your phone?" He gave a curt nod. "Good. Where is it?"

He didn't answer at first, just watched her closely, as if sizing her up. She did the same to him, receiving the full effect of Dr. Thad Markson. Those piercing icy blue eyes and chiseled jaw. The perfectly swept-back dark hair. A hint of stubble beneath the skin of his jaw. His sculpted lips were currently compressed into a thin white line, but she imagined them relaxed, full and soft and...

Whoops. Girl, stop. Now is not the time and he is definitely not the man for you to fantasize about.

Not that she had time for that anyway. Romance was way at the bottom of her to-do list. Especially with a man who practically had a flashing neon sign above his head warning Do Not Touch.

Emma took a deep breath and placed a hand on her hip, waiting for his answer, hoping her inappropriate thoughts did not show on her face.

Finally, Dr. Markson pointed toward a corner of the counter. "On the charger over there."

She turned, mentally shaking off the unwanted fuzzy warmth this man had fizzing inside her like champagne.

You're here to talk about the project. That's it. Get the phone and get on with it.

After getting his phone, she brought it back over to the island so he could unlock it and pull up the app. Dr. Markson cursed under his breath, crimson dotting his high cheekbones, as he scrolled through the screen of information. It was obvious he was embarrassed. She almost felt sorry for the man. Almost.

Their arms accidentally brushed as she sat down on the stool beside his. Zings of awareness raced through her nerve endings while Emma didn't miss how he flinched away from the brief touch.

He shook his head, scowling. "I haven't had an episode that bad in years. I use the latest, best automated insulin delivery system available. Cutting-edge technology. This never should've happened."

"When was the last time you ate?" she asked, clasping her hands in her lap to avoid any accidental brushes against each other again. Dr. Markson clearly didn't like to be touched. Not by her, anyway, if the way he'd pulled back like she'd burned him before was any indication. "Even the best pumps can fail if the patient doesn't follow the proper guidelines."

"I know," he snapped, without glancing at her. "I've been dealing with my condition since I was twelve." He tapped the phone screen a couple of times, then exhaled slowly. "Returning to normal."

"Good."

He set the phone aside and they sat there, silence gathering around them faster than the steady snow blanketing the city outside. Eventually, Dr. Markson hung his head. "I don't want to do your project, Nurse Trudeau. I don't have the time. I'm preparing for a very delicate surgery next month and need to focus all my energy and attention on that."

"It won't take much of your time, actually," she countered, ready for this argument. "I'm prepared to do the bulk of the work. Your connections within the city are what I'm most interested in. To get things going and keep things moving at a steady pace until Christmas Eve. I'll handle the rest."

He did look at her now, all narrowed gaze and pursed lips. Yep. Very kissable indeed. Not that she'd noticed. Nope. Not looking at them at all. "And what makes you think I have connections?"

She almost blurted out the fact that he was rich, but that was rude. Instead, Emma chose her words more carefully. "Your family name is well known in New York. It holds clout with the wealthy and powerful. You have access to people and places I could never approach on behalf of the charity project. Don't you want little Ricky Lynch to get his wish?"

"First of all." He straightened, his color returning. "Do not try to guilt me into participating in your little project, Nurse Trudeau."

"Emma."

Dr. Markson blinked at her, then gave a dismissive wave. "Fine. Whatever. Emma. My point is things have happened in my life you can't even imagine. I understand what Ricky Lynch is going through better than most. Don't ever assume you know me or understand what makes me tick because I can assure you that you don't." He inhaled deep. "And as far as those connections you mentioned, most of them were my father's and I will never, ever use anything that man made. If you'd done your research properly on me in the first place, you'd know why. And you never would've asked me to participate." Slowly, he slid off his stool, as if testing his legs to see if they'd support him. "Now, if you'll excuse me, Everett will show you out."

He was halfway across the kitchen when Emma said, "I know that your father cheated a lot of people out of their money and their homes with his dodgy real estate deals. I know that if he hadn't died five years ago he probably would've been in prison for securities fraud. And you're right. I can't know exactly what it was like growing up with a parent like him. But I did do my research, Dr. Markson. Because I also know you immediately took all the assets your father had left, once he was gone, and set up a foundation to pay restitution to those harmed by your father's actions. I know that you continue that foundation today, even though those affected by your father have long since been compensated and now the foundation funds outreach and all sorts of social welfare programs throughout New York City to better the lives of others. And I know you kept this town house to save it from being torn down and have filed paperwork to have it added to the historic preservation list."

She stood, too, crossing her arms. "Believe me, Dr. Markson. I did my homework, and I understood the assignment. You might be able to intimidate other people at Manhattan West, but I've dealt with far tougher in far worse situations and you won't intimidate me. I've worked too hard for too long to not complete this project. One, because Ricky

Lynch deserves whatever joy he wants for whatever time he has left. And two, because if I get this done—and I will—I have a great shot at a promotion in the ER that will give me more money and a better house and allow me more time to spend with my sister outside of work. So I will camp on your front porch if I must, but we will grant this wish, and you will help me. Do you understand?"

Dr. Markson stood there so long, so still, his back to her, that Emma started to worry maybe he would pass out again. Then, finally, he scrubbed a hand over his face, a bit of the tension in his broad shoulders relaxing as he murmured something to her over his shoulder she didn't catch.

"I'm sorry?" Emma said, stepping closer, in case she needed to catch him before he hit the ground. He was quite a bit bigger than her, but she'd been trained to move large patients without hurting herself, so…

"Thad," he repeated, louder this time. "If we're going to work on this thing together, you should call me Thad. At least here in the town house. Dr. Markson is too formal."

Emma smiled slowly as she did an inner fist pump. Yes. At last she'd made progress here.

Before she could get too excited, though,

he turned to face her again. "I need to eat something." He leaned past her and shouted. "Everett?"

She shook her head. "I can get it for you. I'm already here. What do you want?"

"It's his job," Thad said, frowning and making his way back to his stool at the island, still shakier than Emma would've liked. "Everett likes taking care of me."

"The poor man is probably tired after the ordeal you just put him through." She snorted and got him settled at the island before walking back over to the fridge to peek inside. "How old is your butler, anyway?"

"Seventy-two." He pointed toward the food still strewn across the counters. "I'll just have some toast with peanut butter."

Emma nodded, then raised a brow at him.

"Please," Thad added after a moment.

"Better." Grinning, Emma grabbed the whole-grain bread and jar of peanut butter and carried them over to the toaster sticking out of the carnage. She stuck two slices in, then rested her hips back against the edge of the counter to wait. "You should check your app again. Make sure your numbers are still stable."

Thad scrunched his nose. "Are you always this bossy as a nurse?"

Emma laughed. "Always."

For a second something changed. The tension between them disappeared and he smiled in return, the glory of it shining down on her like the star of Bethlehem. She doubted Thad smiled much, so it was a rare gift indeed. Shame, too, because it was a very nice smile.

Ding!

The toast popped up, breaking her out of her reverie. She pulled it out and spread it with peanut butter before setting two plates on the island, one for him and one for her. At his surprised look, she shrugged. "What? You made me wait so long I missed dinner. I think you owe me a piece of toast. Want something to drink with it, Thad?"

"Cup of tea," he said, almost absently, staring down at his plate like it might blow up any second. "Bags are in the cupboard to the right of the stove. Kettle is on the stove."

She started boiling the water, then searched for cups. He was probably right that calling in the butler would've been easier, but she felt sorry for the older man. Besides, making him food felt like getting to know Thad better. Which she needed to do for the project, not because it felt nice, being here with him and let into his world, however briefly and reluctantly.

His icy gaze still tracked her movements from across the room, sending small shivers of awareness up her spine. He ate a bite of his toast.

In the reflection on the glass door of the microwave over the stove, she caught sight of Thad behind her, running his free hand through his hair, mussing it, and her breath caught. Not just because it was sexy, which it totally was. But also because it made him seem a little less perfect, a little more vulnerable. *Like the rest of us.* Her chest burned with yearning to make him smile again, to see him let his walls down and just be happy for a while. Given all he'd accomplished by the age of thirty-six, he worked hard. Perhaps too hard. Of all people, though, she understood the drive to achieve, and the fear of disappointing those who depended on you. Maybe she and Thad Markson weren't so very different after all?

The kettle whistled, startling Emma. She splashed some milk into the bottom of each cup, then poured the boiling water over the tea bags and carried both cups to the island before taking a seat beside Thad again. Using first names was nice. Friendly. "Maybe now would be a good time to discuss the basics of the project?"

Slowly he lifted the mug to his mouth and took a sip. "Later, please."

Sighing, Emma swallowed a bite of toast. "Okay, but we're already behind on prep because of the Thanksgiving holiday and we can't afford to lose much more time."

Thad looked like he wanted to argue with her, but instead reached down to give his dog a bite of peanut butter toast. "Hey, Baxter," he said, scratching the dog behind the ears. "Good boy."

And there it was. The smile again. This time, Emma had to stop herself from staring and covered it quickly by gulping her tea.

When he straightened again, Thad gave Emma some serious side-eye. "I do believe you'll be nothing but trouble, Emma."

"Trouble's my middle name." She winked up at him, then froze, realizing what she'd done. Flirting wasn't part of the plan, no matter how endearing the man had suddenly become. Baxter the dog came to her rescue then, too, gruffling and wagging his tail, paws prancing on the tile floor in hopes of more treats.

"You've had enough, boy," Thad said, chuckling, the dark timbre of his voice soothing the dog and causing him to lie back down on the floor at Thad's feet. Unfortunately, his tone had a similar effect on Emma, making her heart flip and her entire body sigh with pleasure. If she wasn't careful, she'd end up in a puddle of goo at Thad's feet, just like Baxter. Man, his voice should be bottled and sold like expensive perfume. Intoxicating, sensual, made to whisper naughty things in the deep of the night, then to be followed up with some equally naughty actions.

Stop it!

Alarm bells went off in Emma's head. She had no idea what was wrong with her. She wasn't a woman who swooned over men. Especially ones who were so obviously off-limits. Yet here she was, studying Thad from beneath her lashes as he frowned down into his teacup. From the dark jeans encasing his long legs to the black turtleneck she'd bet her life was made of the finest cashmere and which emphasized the breadth of his shoulders to perfection. Yep. Dr. Thad Markson was a complete stud. Even if most people didn't notice it beneath his churlish demeanor. Even sitting there slumped over his kitchen island, the man exuded a certain power and prowess Emma found intoxicating. She'd always had a thing for competent men, and Thad was the most competent cardiothoracic surgeon in the city. Didn't get more attractive than that for her.

She glanced up at his face again and her throat constricted as her eyes locked with his.

Busted.

"Right." Fresh heat prickled her cheeks and she turned away slightly on her stool to grab her phone from her pocket and pull up the information sheets on Ricky Lynch and his wish she'd received from the charity. She slid her phone over toward Thad so he could see the picture there. "I'll forward these documents to you as well, but this is Ricky Lynch, our wish recipient. He had a brain tumor."

Thad swallowed hard, staring down at the photo of the little boy smiling on her phone screen, his head bald from the chemo. One of his front teeth was missing. He looked too thin, and his skin had a bluish cast. But his eyes still sparkled with life and excitement and reflected back a cheerful happiness remarkable for a kid who'd been through so much in his young life. Beside the boy in his hospital bed was a black Lab with a service dog vest on. Kind of reminded Emma of Baxter.

"What kind of tumor?" Thad asked, his voice gruffer than before.

"Grade four glioblastoma."

Thad winced. "Poor kid."

"Yeah. He was diagnosed at eight. He's nine now. Been in and out of the hospital for the past year. His wish is to have a winter carnival and invite all the kids in the Manhattan West PICU to attend, along with their families."

Thad shifted to look at her phone screen, causing the dog to stir, raising his head to make sure his master didn't disappear on him again. "So, how do we start? I don't know the first thing about carnivals. We'll need a big venue. Those will be hard to come by around the holidays, especially on short notice."

"I'm working on that. It will probably need to be indoors as well since we'll have children with various health conditions there. And ADA accessible too, obviously."

"What about a trip to Disney World?" Thad asked. "We could book him and his family in down there for a week of luxury and fun. Solves all our problems."

She took a deep breath. "I thought that, too, but with his current condition, traveling is impossible. Plus, Ricky wants to share his carnival with his friends in the PICU, so we need to stay here. So I spent this morning calling all the businesses on the list the charity gave me for donations, but with our time constraints, it's going to be hard to get it all together in time."

"Hmm." He frowned. "Sounds like we need a miracle."

Emma sipped her tea, regarding him thoughtfully over the rim. "I don't believe in miracles, Thad. I grew up poor and it taught me to believe in the power of people and their choices. Now, you say you don't know anything about carnivals, but you do have resources. And where there's money, there's a way. I have a list of vendors who are willing to come and can get the booths and rides here before Christmas Eve, barring any bad weather. Maybe your foundation can help coordinate that if you contact them. I'll take care of the organization and invitations and ask for donations from the hospital staff, too. But honestly, you're the only person I know who could pull something like this off. That's why I chose you." From Thad's horrified expression he was ready to bolt again, but she reassured him. "I just want you to see this isn't about waiting for a miracle. It's about working together to put on a winter carnival for Ricky, and all the other sick kids in our PICU. To buy them a few hours of happiness and distraction before they go back to reality, and in some cases, before they are no longer with us. Then you can disappear back into this mansion and your privileged life and never have to hear from me again. All I ask is that you help me now."

She took a deep breath before adding, "This carnival can give something to these kids, something priceless. A memory. A good memory. Something they can pick out, dust off and remember with a smile when things aren't going well. Don't you think they deserve that?" She paused and looked him. "Don't you have memories like that, Thad?"

Emma had a few moments like that to remember: twinkling lights, festive rides, people laughing and having fun. But Thad didn't look like he had any pleasant answers to her question. In fact, when he looked at her at last, his gaze was cold enough to give her frostbite. "No, Emma. I don't."

For a moment she thought about pushing him more but knew it wouldn't get her any further with him. Best to leave things as they were and take the progress she'd made so far tonight. It was getting late, too, and she didn't like leaving Karley alone at night. She stood and smoothed a hand down the front of her beige sweater and jeans. Everett, ever the good butler, was right there with her coat, scarf and hat. "Okay. Well, I think we've made a good start," she said as she tugged on her hat. Not really accurate, but at least she'd sat down with him and talked. That was something. "We, uh, should probably set up our next meeting to plan our next steps. I'm working in the ER tomorrow but can take a break in the afternoon. Say around three. Will that work?"

He took a deep breath, scowling into his tea again. "Fine. But make it three fifteen. I'll find you."

"It's a date," Emma said, then bit her lip when she realized how that sounded. "I mean, not a *date* date, but…"

Stop talking now.

She turned to follow the butler downstairs, but Thad's words stopped her. "If we do this, I want my name kept out of it. Use the foundation's name instead. I'll have my people there do some research on possible venues for us and give you an update tomorrow at our meeting."

It wasn't exactly rousing support, but she'd take it.

"Great." She stood on the threshold of the

kitchen biting back a grin of triumph. "I'll see you tomorrow afternoon."

Things were about to get interesting.

CHAPTER FOUR

"Trauma one, probable UTI," Emma said to one of the residents standing nearby as she stepped out into the hall and closed the curtain behind her. "White blood cell count is twelve thousand, with neutrophils slightly elevated. There's a trace of blood and plus four bacteria in the urine. The patient reports tenderness in the abdomen and in the mid-low back."

The resident nodded, then glanced down the hall toward the nurses' station. "There's, uh, someone here to see you, Nurse Trudeau."

"Who?" Emma frowned. They were slammed today. Nothing major yet, but lots of flu cases and colds. She handed her tablet containing the patient's chart to the resident, then headed toward the nurses' station, checking her smartwatch along the way. Only two thirty, so too early for Thad.

Yet when she rounded the corner, there he

stood, scowling at their assignment board like it was his worst enemy.

Emma sighed. After yesterday, her thinking about him had shifted. Oh, the man was still intimidating, no doubt. At least the rest of the department seemed to think so, seeing how they all gave him a wide berth. But witnessing his vulnerable side in the kitchen the previous night had made a difference for her. She could no longer think of him as just a means to an end to get the charity carnival done. Nope. Growing up, her parents had always warned Emma her soft heart would get her in trouble one day, but it had become one of her greatest assets in her work. Allowing her to understand and empathize with others in a way that built their trust in her and got them to tell her their problems. Of course, she'd learned to put limits on it, too, put up walls to protect herself from those who wanted too much, who drained her energy until there was nothing left. And yes, maybe she'd grown too good at keeping others out over the years, which explained why she was still single at twenty-eight. But Emma was happy with her life and grateful for what she had. Even if what she had at the moment was her partner on the carnival project glaring at her with those icicle-blue eyes.

Despite her wishes, her chest squeezed with unwanted attraction. The man was hot, maybe more so because of his air of cool untouchability. Was it weird to lust after a Grinch? Maybe. Probably.

Get it together, girl.

She shook off the silly thoughts and forced a polite smile. "You're early, Dr. Markson."

"What?" He didn't look away from the board.

"Our meeting isn't until three fifteen, Dr. Markson," Emma said, used to his brusqueness now.

His nose twitched slightly, and he blinked at her, then shook his head. "I'm not here for that. I was called down for a consult on a suspected case of acute decompensated heart failure?"

"Oh." Emma said, focusing on her work and not how handsome he looked in his lab coat. "Okay. Yes, that would be Ms. Lovelace in trauma bay four."

"Right." He started that way, then stopped and said over his shoulder, "I'll need assistance, Nurse Trudeau."

Emma quickly filled in one of the other nurses to help the resident with the UTI, then followed Dr. Markson. Used to Thad's "bedside manner," Emma hurried to enter the patient's room before him and stood by Ms. Lovelace's side to act as a friendly buffer from what she expected to be Thad's more formal exam questions.

Sure enough, Thad started bombarding the older woman the moment he stepped into the room. "You have difficulty breathing and swollen feet. Show me."

Emma cringed on behalf of his less-than-charming social skills and smiled down at the patient. "He's extremely talented as a surgeon."

"He'd better be," the older woman said, shooting Dr. Markson a dubious stare. The woman was a frequent flier in the ER with her dicey insurance situation. Normally thin, tonight Ms. Lovelace looked downright gaunt. From her pinched expression and messy, gray-streaked hair, Emma wondered if she'd been neglecting herself. The woman had no one to care for her; she was in her eighties and not married, nor did she have any children.

While Thad poked and prodded the woman's ankles, Emma tried to discover more about her home situation. "Do you have groceries delivered, Ms. Lovelace? Should I call Meals on Wheels for you?"

"Child, I have all the food I need." The

older woman waved Emma off, her attention laser-focused on Dr. Markson. "What kind of doctor are you again?"

Emma bit back a smile. "He's a heart surgeon."

"Cardiothoracic surgeon," Thad corrected from the end of the bed.

After giving him a look, Emma continued. "He's a specialist who's here to evaluate your heart. Based on your symptoms tonight it sounds like you're having problems again?"

"Lord, yes," Ms. Lovelace huffed. "And I'm so tired all the time."

Thad gave a curt nod. "Fatigue is normal. Three plus pitting edema bilaterally." He next moved to the patient's chest, using his stethoscope to listen to her breathing.

"Damn, son!" Ms. Lovelace scowled up at him. "Warn a lady about your cold hands, why don't ya?"

This time Emma coughed to cover her laugh. Leave it to the elderly to tell it like it was.

"What about water, Ms. Lovelace?" Emma asked, walking to the keyboard in the corner to pull up the patient's file and enter the vitals Thad gave her. "Last time you were in, I believe the resident had ordered you to drink at least sixty-four ounces a day."

"Well, I'm not." The older woman sighed. "I mean, I do drink when I'm thirsty, but then I have to go to the bathroom more and it's hard for me to get around. Plus, I'm not sleeping well at night, so sometimes I fall asleep during the day and miss meals. Which is just as well because the charity group that used to bring me food every month is low on donations, so they can only come every other month now. Sometimes I catch my neighbor when he goes to work but his hours are odd and I don't always get him."

Emma typed all that in, along with the other findings Thad called out to her like they'd been a team forever.

"And when did the breathing issues worsen?" Thad asked, straightening at last.

"Two nights ago," Ms. Lovelace said. "At first, I thought it was bronchitis messing with my lungs again, but this morning I couldn't catch my breath."

Thad walked out of the room without another word, leaving Emma to make apologies before chasing after him.

As she hurried down the hall, Emma didn't miss the looks both she and Thad received from the staff, including Emma's best friend, another nurse named Danielle. Emma had told Dani about the project and her plans to recruit Dr. Markson. Now though, she was regretting letting her bestie in on the secret, based on Dani's too-inquisitive stare.

"What are your orders, Dr. Markson?" Emma asked once they'd stopped at the nurses' station again.

"The immediate goal is to reestablish adequate perfusion and oxygen delivery to the patient's organs," he said, as if just now noticing that Emma was there. Laser focus. It's what made him such a brilliant surgeon, and such a pain in the butt to wrangle. "Prop the patient's head up, give her oxygen, morphine if she's in pain, IV Lasix and enalapril, along with some nitrates and digoxin for the slight arrhythmia I detected on exam. If that doesn't work, we'll look at more drastic interventions."

"Drastic measures?" Emma only knew the patient through the ER, but still she cared.

"Yes." He washed his hands in the sink nearby while Emma typed the orders into the computer. "If it turns out her kidneys are failing, then we'll need to handle that issue as well."

Emma swallowed hard. Kidney failure would mean dialysis, which would mean regular trips to a clinic and more burden on poor Ms. Lovelace. She was so caught up in her thoughts, she didn't even realize he'd come up behind her until he spoke, his warm breath near her ear making her shiver.

"I don't expect it's that bad though," he said, his voice low and deep, intimate, for her ears only. "Also, thank you for assisting me in there, Emma."

"You're welcome," she squeaked out past her constricted vocal cords, turning slightly to look at him over her shoulder. He was close, so close that if there hadn't been people around and she'd been braver, she could've risen on tiptoe and kissed him. He smiled then, teeth even and white, lips soft and sinfully sexy, and...

Oh, boy.

Emma turned back around fast, cheeks hot and mouth dry. "I'll keep you updated on the patient's progress."

"Perfect." Thad walked away, seemingly oblivious to the fact he'd just rocked Emma's world. "See you at three fifteen, Nurse Trudeau."

But unfortunately, fate had other ideas, because the busy ER got busier and Emma and Thad were thrown together again on a case, this time an overweight man with a sharp tightness in his chest. When she'd offered to have one of the residents take the case instead, Thad had brushed her off.

"I'm the only one in my department, and I like to stay busy," he said, like that covered it. As far as Emma knew, Thad normally avoided her department like an Ebola outbreak, but suddenly he was around today. A lot. With her. She didn't want to think too hard about why that was occurring because honestly, they were short-staffed and could use all the help they could get today. She and Thad worked on the obese patient, doing an EKG, which showed left ventricular hypertrophy and a possible blockage. They stabilized the man while awaiting the results of his cardiac enzyme tests.

"I've read your chest X-ray, Mr. Trotter," Thad said to the patient about twenty minutes later. "And your heart is enlarged. Part of that is due to your high blood pressure and congestive heart failure, but you still shouldn't have the chest pain. One of the heart enzymes in your blood, called troponin, is elevated, suggesting your heart muscle isn't getting enough oxygen. So—" he turned then to Emma "—let's get the patient moved up to the cardiac-care unit for closer observation. And schedule a cardiac catheterization in the morning. That way, if there are any blockages, I can repair them immediately."

Emma prepared the transfer information while Thad answered questions from the man's wife. By then it was nearly time for Emma's break and their meeting. She finished up with Mr. Trotter and his wife before clocking out and going downstairs to the basement cafeteria with Thad to discuss the carnival plans in private.

She settled at a table in the corner to wait for Thad while he got his drink and pulled out her phone to take notes on their project updates. When he finally sat down, though, he had a whole tray of food.

He put a napkin on her lap, then looked up at her. "What? It's time for me to eat and I didn't want to be rude by doing it in front of you. So I got enough for two. Wasn't sure what you liked. Vegetarian? Gluten free? Pescatarian? Vegan? There's a bit of everything."

"Oh. Um." She shook her head. "I'm not on any special diet, but thanks. I guess."

"You're welcome." His voice once again stroked against her skin like velvet and Emma battled another shudder of awareness from rippling through her. They were here to discuss their progress on the carnival, not for her to drool all over him. She sat back and refocused on her notes rather than her inappropriate attraction to Thad.

"Here." He passed her an unopened bag of pita chips before digging into his chicken Caesar salad. "Eat those."

"I'm not really hungry," she said, setting the bag aside.

"What time did your shift start to day?" he asked between bites of food.

"Seven this morning. Why?"

"And when did you last eat?"

Emma had to think about that for a second. "Dinner last night. But I had a whole burger and fries, so I'm still full."

He snorted, then shook his head. "You need to take the same level of care with yourself as you do for others."

"I…" Emma frowned. She took care of herself. She ate well, or tried to, between her busy work schedule and Karley's school activities. And she certainly got enough exercise running around the ER all day. Defensive, she tried again to get their meeting back on track. "We're here to talk about the project."

"Do you always do that?"

"What?"

"Deflect away from yourself?" Thad wiped

his mouth on his napkin, then narrowed his gaze. "You don't like being in the spotlight."

"I have no problem—"

"It wasn't a question," he said, cutting her off. "You prefer to let others shine. I see it very clearly."

"Do you?" Heat prickling her face, she compressed her lips. The fact that his words had hit far too close to home only unsettled her more. Part of her wanted to tell him where to go and how to get off, but the other part of her felt far too exposed and raw. She didn't like being the center of attention, it was true. But that was a good thing, right? Her sister didn't agree. Karley was always on at Emma to stand up for herself, to toot her own horn, as Karley called it. Maybe if she did, Emma still wouldn't be waiting for a promotion that was long overdue by any standards. But she felt more comfortable in the background. Not that she would let Thad Markson know it, though. She raised her chin and waggled her phone between her fingers. "I've only got twenty minutes left on my break and we have a lot to do. And if we're going to talk about people's life choices, why are you being so nice to me all of a sudden, bringing me lunch? Yesterday you wanted nothing to do with me."

Thad gave a slight shrug, then ate another bite of salad. "I don't like to eat alone."

"But you live alone."

"Everett is there."

"Does your butler eat with you?" Emma found that hard to believe.

"Sometimes," Thad said, surprising her. She couldn't imagine the staid older man breaking protocol like that. "And there's Baxter, too…"

And damn. Now he'd gone and made her feel sorry for him again. She resisted the urge to rub the sore spot on her chest over her heart as she pictured Thad eating alone at the granite island in his massive kitchen. Apparently, that old adage was right. Money wasn't everything. Distracted, she reached for her bag of chips and accidentally brushed her hand against Thad's free one on the table. Her nerve endings zinged, but this time Thad didn't pull away fast as he had before. Their eyes met and she saw the same shocked awareness she felt in his gaze.

Oh boy.

Emma opened the chips and popped one in her mouth, looking away fast. And yeah. Fine. She was kind of hungry.

"How old are you?" Thad blurted out, his expression unreadable.

"Uh." She frowned. "First of all, that's rude. And second, twenty-eight. How old are you?"

"Thirty-six." He pushed away his now-empty salad plate before starting on a bowl of yogurt with blueberries. "Have you always lived in New York?"

"Yes." Emma exhaled slowly and ate another chip, losing hope for their planning session. "You?"

"Same," He stared into his yogurt. "What made you want to be a nurse?"

"I didn't have time for medical school." She devoured a few more chips and at his curious look, continued. "My parents were killed in a car accident when I turned eighteen. I had a full scholarship for a pre-med program, but with my little sister to raise there was no time. And I had to bring in income to keep a roof over our heads. So I put aside my dreams of being a doctor and went to community college at night instead, so I could hold down a full-time job to support us. Took me longer than I wanted to graduate, but I got there. Got a job here at Manhattan West after graduation and worked my way up."

Everyone reacted differently to her story. Some pitied her. Some applauded her gumption. Rarely, though, did Emma feel like anyone really saw her. Not her looks or skin color or tragic past, but her.

But when Thad looked at her, she felt seen. Right down to her core. So much so she had to fight not to squirm. It was uncomfortable and unsettling and more than a little unbelievable. Because of course it would be the one man she could never imagine herself with in a million years who finally got her.

Silence stretched taut between them until he finally changed the subject. "Tell me what you've done so far on your plans."

While she told him about the vendor calls she'd made that morning, Thad wrestled with his rioting emotions. He wasn't sure what he'd expected Emma's life and past to be like, but he hadn't been prepared for her truth. Even with his own mother dying when he was just ten from cancer and living with his cold, distant father afterward, Thad knew his life had been privileged.

But hearing her speak about losing her dream of becoming a doctor because of such horrible circumstances and the choices she'd been forced to make to survive, well… Thad swallowed hard. It was heartbreaking. Still, she managed to remain upbeat, optimistic, happy despite the scars grief inevitably left inside you. She'd persevered, finding new opportunities to move forward when others closed on her. She'd turned her troubles into triumphs and damn if Thad didn't admire Emma for it.

And now she'd turned that same dogged determination to helping a sad, sick little boy get his dream come true. He remembered the image of little Ricky Lynch from the project brief, clutching the neck of his service dog. A dog who looked remarkably like Baxter. And that dog wasn't the only thing he and Ricky had in common, either. Thad had spent more than enough time in hospitals as a kid. Scared and lonely and sick as they'd worked to regulate his diabetes. Sometimes, if he closed his eyes, he could still hear the beep of monitors and smell the disinfectant.

"Thad?" Emma asked, jarring him back to the present.

He started, blinking at her, the sound of his name on her lips still ringing in his ears—sweet and soft and a tad sultry. Deep inside him, something tightly coiled unfurled. "Yes?"

She looked concerned. "Everything okay?"

Thad resorted to his usual brusque business mode again, same as he always did when he felt too raw. "Fine. I think we need to consider the venue carefully, given we're dealing with extremely ill children here. Can't have them traipsing about outside in the snow and freezing temperatures. I need to do more research to find a suitable location."

He kept his eyes locked on his yogurt bowl the whole time to avoid gazing at Emma like some smitten schoolboy. It was ridiculous. He was never besotted. He was a Markson, for God's sake.

"Agreed," she said, tapping her phone screen. "I thought about that, too. But it will need to be a pretty big venue for all the rides and booths and things. Plus have good ventilation and access to bathrooms. Not easy to find this close to Christmas."

After considering that a moment, Thad said, "I've got my foundation on it. They should get back to me soon with a report." At her expectant look, his pulse tripped. He'd grown up seeing his father throw his financial weight around and the consequences of that with his shady real estate deals had not been good. People had lost their homes, their life savings, because of his father. Thad was hesitant to do anything even remotely similar to his father's, using money and influence to push things through he wanted, but this was for a good cause and Emma had him fired up. "And I'll make some calls too. See if I can move them along any faster." He finished his yogurt, then stacked his things back on the tray. "I'll try and coordinate the mechanics of the rides as well, since you already started on the vendor list. What should we get? Ferris wheel, Scrambler, fun house? Maybe a bouncy house or fun slide?"

"A Ferris wheel might be hard to fit indoors." Emma practically beamed at him now and Thad found himself enchanted. "Maybe something smaller. Like a carousel?"

"Is that your favorite ride?" He wasn't sure why he'd asked, but it seemed important he know.

"It is." Her bright smile faltered before she looked away. "I remember riding one with my parents as a kid. Everyone was so happy and carefree."

He studied her wistful expression, her smooth skin and lovely dark eyes and those lips, so soft and kissable and...

Whoops. No.

Thad shoved those thoughts from his head and forced himself to get up and throw his trash away instead before they headed back to work. At the elevators, Emma yawned and stretched, her blue scrub top riding up slightly to reveal a sliver of bare skin at her waist. Thad looked away fast, throat tight.

"I think we got a good start," he said, his voice gruff to his own ears.

"We did." The elevator dinged and Emma stepped on board, holding the door for him. "I'll text you with our next meeting time?"

"Yes. Good." He cleared his throat, clasping his hands behind his back and staring straight ahead. "And thank you for helping me last night in my kitchen." Uncomfortable heat climbed his neck from beneath the starched collar of his dress shirt. "I look forward to your text."

The elevator dinged and the doors opened on the first floor. Emma got off, then turned to look at him. "You're welcome, about the kitchen thing last night. And thanks for the chips."

Neither moved. Thad held the doors until they beeped.

"So—" Emma stared.

"Maybe—" Thad said at the same time.

Both laughed. Then Thad said, "You go first."

"I was thinking we should meet Ricky in person. Tell him what we're planning and see if he has any more ideas we should incorporate. Maybe one day next week?" Her cheeks flushed a pink and she stared down at her toes. "If you're available."

"Yes." He cleared his throat. "I'm free on Wednesday around lunchtime."

"Good. Me, too." Thad felt her answering grin like the sun breaking through a cloudy day. "Next Wednesday it is."

CHAPTER FIVE

As soon as they arrived on the sixth floor of Manhattan West the following week, it was like being in another world. Like being home, in a weird way. Children's wards were one of the few places, beside the OR, where Thad felt entirely relaxed, entirely himself. Here the temperature was different, the mood was different. Even the lighting was different. Everything felt softer, warmer, kinder. Even if it was all just an illusion.

Several huge Christmas trees dotted the floor. One near the elevators at the entrance. Another at the end of the main corridor. And yet another still filled a corner of the kids' playroom, its colorful decorations creating a rainbow effect. Beneath each tree awaited a bevy of wrapped gifts for their small patients, brought by family and friends and staff. Paintings made by the kids in the ward decorated the walls with Santa and reindeer and snowmen in all shapes and sizes. And even the kids in isolation because of infection risk had fiber-optic trees outside their windows in the hallway, the ever-changing lights reflecting joyfully back inside their rooms. The staff in the PICU bent over backward to make each child feel special at this time of year.

They always had.

Chest tight, Thad stepped up to the desk at the nurses' station and cleared his throat. "I'm Dr. Markson and this is Nurse Emma Trudeau. We're here to see Ricky Lynch."

The middle-aged Latina woman behind the desk whose name tag read Perla smiled wide. "He's been waiting for you two to arrive." She looked from Thad to Emma. "You work down in the ER, right? I think you helped me a month or so ago when I had to bring my mom in."

"I do." Emma smiled back. "And I remember you now. How's your mother doing?"

"Much better, thanks. We finally got her blood pressure regulated, which was a big deal. She's also on a special diet and moving more, so she's doing really good." Perla finished typing something on her computer, then stood. "Right. Let's go see Ricky. Follow me."

The atmosphere here was the opposite to what Thad was used to in the high-pressure, competitive world of specialist surgery. Staff in the PICU never held any airs or graces. Never jockeyed for position or shouted orders at one another. In fact, at one time, Thad had considered going into pediatric surgery instead of his chosen field. But that was not good enough for his father, who had always insisted Thad be the best, do the best, have the best, or else he was worthless. Being back in such a gentle, soothing, supportive environment now felt like an opposite universe from what Thad had become familiar with growing up with his horrible father. Still, a part of him deep inside remembered this place, and a tiny sprout of warmth broke through the hardened soil of his soul. Perhaps his heart wasn't completely dead after all.

Perla pointed toward the end of the main corridor. "Ricky's in room three. His parents are working today but left word for you to go on in and speak with their son. Oh, and McCoy's in there too."

"McCoy?" Thad frowned.

"His emotional support dog," Perla said, her expression a bit sad. "Helps him deal with things."

"Right. Thank you." Thad started down

the hall. The floor had been updated since his last stay there as a child, but he still remembered the layout. Emma followed behind him, oddly quiet.

Thad slowly opened the door to the room in case Ricky had fallen asleep so as not to disturb him. Chemotherapy and radiation tended to zap all of a person's energy. But when he peeked inside, the young boy was wide-awake, talking to the large Lab on his bed. The sprout of emotion in his heart grew larger, choking the air from his lungs. Baxter meant so much to Thad now, the unconditional love and support of an animal. Back when he'd been Ricky's age and stuck in here, with no one to visit him except Everett, Thad would've given anything to have a friend like McCoy by his side.

Both Ricky and the dog looked over as Thad and Emma entered, the dog whimpering slightly because they were strangers. Ricky looked the same as he had in the photo from the project brief. Bald from the chemo, skin so pale it was almost translucent and blue. But a smile so wide and earnest it made Thad's newly resuscitated heart ache.

"Hello, Ricky," Thad said, his voice a tad gruffer than normal. "We're here to talk about your wish."

Ricky's blue eyes sparkled with excitement. "Yay!"

"My name's Dr. Markson, but you can call me Thad." He stood beside him. "And this is Nurse Trudeau."

"Emma," she said. "May I pet your dog?"

"Sure, Emma," Ricky said, grinning at the Lab. "McCoy loves attention."

They both greeted the dog, then pulled up chairs to the boy's bedside. "Now, about the carnival you wished for," Thad started.

"I want cake," Ricky said, tossing away the covers and throwing his legs over the side of his bed.

"Cake?" Thad frowned. "We didn't bring any cake."

"No, silly." Ricky shook his head. "There's cake in the TV room. Come on, McCoy."

The dog jumped down, trailing along beside the boy, nudging Ricky's hand with his wet nose to let him know he was there, much as Baxter did to Thad. The boy stopped at the door and gestured to them. "You want cake, too? I'm sure there's enough."

Emma shrugged, then glanced at Thad. "Cake sounds good to me."

They went back down the corridor to a room with several round tables in it and a large flat-screen TV on the wall showing

cartoons. On another table against the wall
the staff had set out plates of cookies and
bottles of drinks and a large sheet cake in
the shape of a rocket. Emma got Ricky and
McCoy settled, then joined Thad near the
refreshments.

"Wow," she said, scanning the assortment
of stuff. "This is quite a spread. I wonder
if it was someone's birthday or something."

"I doubt it." Thad shrugged. "They usually keep some kind of food around at all
times in this ward. Some of the kids can't
eat at usual mealtimes because of their treat-
ments. Most of the time it's healthy snacks
like veggies or granola or fruit. But considering the state some of these children are in
health-wise, they can be lenient, too, and give
them sweets as well to keep them happy." He
picked up a plate and filled it with fresh veggies and hummus while Emma grabbed some
cake for herself and Ricky. "If the patient is
midway through chemo and can't face regular food the staff will give them anything
they want to get some calories in them. I remember when I was in here one time, a nurse
made a mad dash at midnight just to find a
kid the kind of candy bar he craved."

The minute he said the words, Thad froze.
He hadn't meant to share so much with

Emma. Gaze trained on his plate, he added a few whole-grain crackers to his assortment of healthy snacks, hoping perhaps she hadn't heard him.

No such luck.

"Do you spend a lot of time up here now?" Emma asked, her intense gaze burning a hole through the side of his head. "Or was this when you were a child?"

Thad grabbed a bottled water. "It was a long time ago."

Emma looked like she wanted to ask more, but Thad stopped her. "Please not now. We're here for Ricky. He's having a good day and I don't want to spoil that by focusing on me and my past."

Before she could respond, he rejoined the boy at the table. Emma followed and soon they were discussing everything about the carnival.

Ricky seemed very chatty, asking lots of questions while slipping McCoy bites of his vanilla cake with strawberry frosting. "What about pony rides?"

"No pony rides. Too many health concerns and regulations," Thad said. He felt for the kid, but there were limits. "Not to mention the cleanup and waste—"

"We're thinking games instead, Ricky,"

Emma intervened, giving Thad a look. "All free with prizes, even if you didn't win."

"Oh, I love prizes!" Ricky clapped and wriggled in his seat a little. "What kind of prizes?"

While Emma and the boy discussed the toy options, Thad ate his veggies and marveled at how good she was with people. His mom had been great with people, too. But Thad had never learned that skill. First because of his isolated childhood after his mother's death, and later because he valued his privacy far more than the risks of social interaction. Of course, he knew people complained about his bedside manner, but once his patients recovered from things others had said were impossible to cure, they forgot about his terseness soon enough. And yes, maybe he did feel lonely sometimes, even with Everett and Baxter there for company. Everyone got lonely. It was fine. All fine.

Normal part of life. Had nothing to do with the sudden appearance of Emma Trudeau in his life or the odd sparks of emotion bursting forth like fireworks inside him whenever she was around. It would pass. It always did.

After about an hour, Ricky yawned and sagged in his chair, pushing his empty plate away. "I think I need a nap now."

They quickly cleaned up their table, then walked the boy back to his room, making sure he was warm and comfortable in his bed with the dog by his side before Thad and Emma made their way back out to the elevators in the lobby. But instead of leaving right away, she led him over to some chairs behind the large Christmas tree. Thad figured she wanted to go over what they'd learned from Ricky about the carnival, but instead she patted the seat beside her and looked up at him.

"Tell me about being in this place as a child."

Thad frowned, his guard up. "Why? It has no bearing on what we're doing here."

"It could," Emma argued. "You have personal insight into what these children go through in here. We could use that to make our carnival even more fun for them."

"I don't see how," he groused, reluctantly sitting beside her. This. This was exactly why he didn't talk to people, open up to them. Because they wanted more. Always more. Poking and prodding and making him feel raw and vulnerable and like he was right back in the dark corners he used to hide in as a child to avoid the wrath of his father and later the intrusiveness of the press and anger of the people his father had cheated. He'd repaid them all, every last cent, and still they continued to hound his foundation. No. Letting people in only meant they could hurt you. His father had taught him that lesson well.

But from the determined expression Emma wore, she wasn't letting this go until he told her something. Thad sighed and squeezed the bridge of his nose between his thumb and forefinger. "Fine. What do you want to know exactly?"

"Were you here because of your diabetes?"

"Yes." He hoped that one-word answer would suffice. It did not. She continued to stare at him until he continued. "Why are we doing this, Emma? I really don't think it will help with the project at all and I'm not comfortable talking about myself."

"Because of your family."

"Because of a lot of things."

They sat there in silence for a while, staring at the massive tree in front of them. Finally, Emma huffed out a breath. "I thought talking about ourselves might make working on the project go more smoothly, that's all." She shrugged. "How about we try a different topic. One not quite so personal? Tell me why you don't like Christmas."

Thad hid a wince, barely. In truth, that question was even more personal than the first one she'd asked. He tried to deflect instead. "I never said I don't like Christmas."

"Seriously?" she snorted, raising one brow. "You know they call you the Fifth Avenue Grinch, right?"

He gave her a side glance. "How childish." *How true.*

Thad's chest squeezed tight with old pain. As a skinny kid who'd had to check his blood sugar often, he'd been bullied a lot and had the inner scars to prove it. But considering what else he'd been called in his life, especially by his own father, Thad figured a Grinch wasn't so bad.

She sighed and looked over at him again. "But it's not true. You're..."

"I'm what?" He gave her a deadpan stare.

"Complicated."

He pressed his lips together to stifle a smile. Complicated. He could live with that.

They watched the tree some more, the lights twinkling and ornaments sparkling. It wasn't often that Thad spent time doing nothing, but it was rather...nice. He was on call, but otherwise there wasn't anything pressing he needed to get to, other than home.

"So," Emma tried again. "What is it about the holidays that bothers you so much?"

"Besides the commercialism?" Thad took a deep breath. "Why do you care so much?"

"Because I—"

He shook his head. "Forget I asked."

She was always so ready to talk, so ready to open herself to anyone who asked, that it made Thad frightened for her. Hadn't anyone told her of the dangers of letting people in, letting them close? It brought out a strange protectiveness in him, wanting to keep her safe from anyone who'd harm her. Weird that. The only other people he felt that way toward were Everett and his dog Baxter. And his late mother. But she was looking at him again, watching him, and those darned fireworks were bursting in his stomach, urging him to tell her something, to make her happy, so he blurted out, "Something bad happened to me a long time ago around Christmas, so that's why I hate the holiday."

"Oh, Thad." Emma reached over and took his hand, shocking the hell out of him. "I'm so sorry. Christmas can be rough for so many people. If there's anything I can do—"

"Unless you can bring back my dead mother, there isn't." He tried to tug his hand free from her, embarrassed and raw from saying way more than he'd intended. He never talked about his mother's death anymore. Thad had buried it so deep he rarely thought about it. He'd thought he'd put it all well and truly behind him, but apparently not. What was it about this woman that unearthed all these painful things inside him and brought them rushing to the surface? Emma didn't say anything more, just sat there, holding Thad's hand while he battled the roiling emotions inside him for control. Fierce grief, fresh as the day he'd lost his mother, clawed his throat, making it burn. He blinked at the tree, forcing the words out before they choked him. "I was ten when she died of cancer. It all happened so quick. Six months from diagnosis to death. There was no time to process, no time to prepare."

There. He'd answered her question; now they could get up and get out of here.

Except his heart pounded against his rib cage like it wanted to escape. His temples throbbed and his gut knotted. Thad stared at the tree again as he returned to the awful day of her passing. Christmas. A time when the whole world rejoiced. But not the Markson residence. In his mind, Thad still heard the ringing phone, the sound of his father's voice as they'd told him his wife was gone, the smell of coffee and raw anguish curdling the air. "She was only thirty-eight. Too young."

"Oh, Thad." Emma's voice caught on a sob and she squeezed his hand, her skin warm against his chilled fingers. "I'm so sorry. I didn't realize or I never would've asked."

Without thinking, he found himself turning his hand over to entwine their fingers, the need to comfort her, too, suddenly overwhelming. "I associate the holiday with her death. All the decorations, all the people so happy, only reminds me of what I lost. My mother, the center of my universe." His face twisted slightly. "My father went downhill after that, too."

Part of him screamed for him to stop talking, stop spilling all his secrets to this woman he barely knew, but Thad couldn't seem to stop himself. There was something about Emma that made him want to open up, want to be vulnerable. It both terrified and tempted him to do more, be more, with her.

Another small eternity of silent seconds passed before she scooted slightly in her seat to face him, reaching up slowly to smooth the hair at his temple. "Thank you for telling me that, Thad. I know it wasn't easy for you and I appreciate your trust."

Trust? Thad looked at her then, as if seeing her for the first time, this woman who'd crashed into his life out of nowhere and somehow, suddenly made it…better. For the first time it dawned on him, that yes, he did trust her. As much as he trusted anyone these days. But there was still so much about her that was a mystery. He'd been vulnerable, now it was her turn. "What about you?"

"What about me? I love Christmas. Obviously," she smiled and sat back, her hand falling away from his face. Thad missed the touch immediately.

"No, I mean what was it like raising your younger sibling?" Now that Thad had started asking about her past, he couldn't seem to stop. "Do you resent having to give up your dreams for her?"

"What? No. Of course I don't resent Karley." Emma frowned. "She's my sister and I love her. We're the only family each of us has left. We have to stick together. The accident that killed our parents wasn't her fault. She was only seven at the time."

He nodded. "Still, it must've been hard for you. Thinking about what might have been."

She crossed her arms and scowled at the tree. "Not really. Honestly, I don't think like that."

"How can you not?"

"Because it's a luxury we couldn't afford. At eighteen, I had to step up to the plate and be the adult. I couldn't sit around wallowing and feeling sorry for myself." She shook her head. "Don't get me wrong. I still grieved. Hell, sometimes I still cry for my parents because I miss them, especially this time of year. But I had to keep moving forward for Karley's sake. To take care of her and to set a good example."

"Eleven years is a big age gap between kids," he said, doing the calculations in his head, way more interested in Emma's life than he'd let himself be in another person's in a long time. "Did your parents plan it that way?"

"Not really." She smiled and glanced over at him. "They tried for a while to have another kid, but it just didn't work out. Then, one day, when they'd stopped trying…there came Karley."

"Huh."

"Yeah. Funny how things work out sometimes, isn't it?" she asked, smiling at him again.

That tug of connection Thad felt for her tugged tighter. "How do you do it?"

Emma gave him a puzzled look. "Do what?"

"How do you remain so positive when you've lost so much in your life?"

She took a moment, then shrugged. "I mean everyone loses something in life eventually, right? It's how we choose how to deal with it that matters. I guess I choose to be happy."

Thad couldn't look away from her, his chest buzzing with warmth and compassion for this brave, beautiful woman who'd stepped in when no one else could. First for her sister, then with him. They were close now, so close her warmth breath fanned his face. He heard a catch when she inhaled and saw her pink lips part, and his long-dead heart jumped with excitement, swelling bigger in his constricted chest until he thought he might die from the sheer anticipation. He closed his eyes, whether to sear this memory into his brain or because it felt like too much, too soon, he wasn't sure. Whispered her name like a prayer, "Emma."

Then suddenly they kissed. He wasn't sure who leaned into whom, but Thad couldn't get enough. He cupped her cheeks, her skin silky and hot beneath his fingertips. Emma stilled at first, then clutched his shirt, right over his heart, in her fist, keeping him right where he was. Time slowed and the world narrowed to only them, only now, only this kiss.

Ding!

The elevator doors nearby *whooshed* open, reminding him of where they were, who they were. Thad pulled back, resting his forehead against Emma's, their rapid breaths still mingling between parted lips.

What the hell am I doing?

Unfortunately, Thad had no answer to that question because he had no clue. Disoriented and unsettled, his skin felt too tight for his body. But he couldn't let her go. Not yet.

Neither moved nor spoke for a long while, hidden behind the tree. Until, at last, Thad sat back, inhaling some much-needed oxygen. Words stuck in his throat, which was probably good because he feared anything he said right then would sound ridiculous. Kissing Emma made no sense. Neither did telling her about his past. But he didn't regret it. Not yet anyway. He stared down at his hands in his lap and managed to croak out, "Thank you for setting this up today."

"Of course," she murmured, looking anywhere but at him, seemingly as flustered as him. "Ricky's a great kid. I'm glad we can make his wish come true."

You could make my wish come true.

And if that wasn't a sign to get the hell out of there, Thad didn't know what was.

He stood fast and raked a hand through

his hair. "We should…uh…" *Stop stammering, idiot!* His father's cold voice resonated through Thad's head. "We should go."

Emma nodded and stood, following him to the elevators. "Yeah. I guess we should."

Thad spent the rest of the ride down to the first floor berating himself. All his good intentions, all the barriers he'd spent years building around his life, his heart. All thrown out the window over one kiss. Was it worth it? His newly awakened heart said yes. But his mind, ever wary, wasn't so sure at all.

Restless after she left Manhattan West, Emma wasn't ready to go home yet, even though she had the day off. She needed some time and some space to think about everything that had happened in the PICU, especially the kiss with Thad. It was warmer today and sunny, so she got on a train for Brooklyn and decided to stop by the cemetery to see her parents.

She got off at the Ninth Avenue station and stopped at a street vendor to buy two small pretty poinsettia wreaths, then headed across the street into Green-Wood. The place was peaceful, as always, a tiny oasis in the chaos that was Brooklyn. A layer of freshly fallen snow covered the ground and many

of the historical markers there. Her parents
had loved this place when Emma was little
and had brought her there often for walks
in the summer, pointing out graves from
the Revolutionary War onward. Some were
huge and ornate, others small and quiet. But
all marked lives that had been important to
someone. They had outdoor concerts here in
the spring and summer, too, and there was
even a public art exhibit here, where people
could write their innermost secrets and put
the note through a slot in the special head
stone to help them release whatever was trou-
bling them.

Emma followed the trails through the huge
478-acre park, passing the frozen pond and
gorgeous sculptures, until she reached the
little ridge where her parents rested side by
side. She placed the wreaths on their head-
stone and cleared the snow from atop the
granite marker, then took a seat on the little
bench nearby. She'd come here at least once
a month—sometimes with her sister, sometimes separately—since they'd died, just to
talk to them and clear her head and heart.
Today was no different.

Sounds of the winter birds and the distant
clop of horses' hooves from the carriages
that ran through the cemetery lulled her into

a more meditative state. She smiled softly at her parents' graves and said quietly, "Hello. It's me. Back again."

Some people might think it was silly, talking to dead loved ones, but Emma found it comforting. Like they were still there, looking out for her even though she couldn't see them.

"Things are going well," she said, nudging the snow with the toe of her boot. "Karley's applying for colleges. Fingers crossed she gets into Howard this fall."

Hushed voices nearby had her glancing up to see a small group of people walking by on a tour. She waited until they'd passed, then turned to her parents again. "Work's been busy," she said. "I'm working on a special project. Granting a Christmas wish for a sick child." She huffed out a laugh, the sound frosting on the air. "I have a partner. His name is Thad. He's…different." Emma thought about that for a second. "Surprising. Maybe that's a better word."

Yep. Thad had surprised her all right. And it wasn't just the kiss earlier, either. Though that had been something. Sitting here, her lips still tingled. She raised a mittened hand to them, remembering the feel of his mouth on hers, the warmth of his nearness, the soft flick of his tongue against hers.

Heat prickled her cheeks despite the cold temperatures.

Other things about Thad surprised her, too. She'd always had this vision of how wealthy people lived, formed mainly through what she'd seen on TV and in social media. That they had entourages and people around to do their bidding. But Thad had money, lots of it if the town house was anything to go by, and yet he lived quietly and alone. Other than the dog and Everett.

But the most surprising thing about Thad was how vulnerable he was just below his tough surface. Not only because of his illness, but also all the things he'd been through. He kept most people at bay and the fact he'd let her in felt, well, special. It pulled at her heartstrings, which both terrified and thrilled her. For a woman who'd done it all on her own for so long, could she afford to let him in now?

"Do I want to?" she asked aloud.

She realized she did. She liked Thad Markson. He was bright and interesting and sometimes stubborn to a fault, but then wasn't everyone. He could be an ass, but he could also be immensely kind and caring, too. He saved lives. He needed saving himself.

Emma. If she closed her eyes, she could still him whispering her name, so much hope and hesitation there. She felt the same emotions coursing through her, too, about him.

A gentle wind rustled through the bare tree branches above her, and one lonely leaf fell, bright red, into her lap, like a sign from above. She chuckled and picked it up, holding it out toward her parents' heads one. "Is this supposed to be a sign?"

"Tweet, tweet," a bright red cardinal chirped from atop a cross on the graves next door.

Red had been her mom's favorite color, too.

And while Emma wasn't a member of any particular religion she considered herself quite spiritual and took a hint when one was given. "Okay. Fine. I do like him. Probably more than I should. Not that I'll go crazy over him because that's not me. But I might give him a chance. See what happens."

"Tweet, tweet!" the cardinal said before flying away, as if his mission was done here.

Emma smiled and snuggled down in her coat, standing to straighten the wreaths once more before stepping back. "Well, I should go. It's cold out here and I need to get home to Karley. I'll come back around the holidays. Love you both and miss you."

She blew them kisses, then headed on toward the exit, underneath the massive Gothic archway, leaving the haven of Green-Wood and walking toward home. She didn't have many more answers than when she'd started, but she felt more settled, as if she had guardian angels on her shoulders, watching out for her.

Thad was a puzzle, wrapped in an enigma. Each layer she peeled back revealed another. But the longer she spent with him, the more she wanted to know him. And if they kissed again? Well, she wasn't the type to make out with virtual strangers, but there was something between them—warm and precious and unexpectedly real—and she wasn't ready to close the door on that special gift just yet.

CHAPTER SIX

SATURDAY AFTERNOON, Thad stood at the window in the study behind his desk and stared out at south Central Park. In the distance he could see Wollman Rink, and dots of red and blue skating around on it. Then there was Heckscher Playground, the ball diamonds covered in tarps and snow now. And the octagonal building housing the historic carousel from the earlier 1900s. Back when he'd been younger, Thad had spent many a long hour up here, watching all the other children play while he was stuck inside studying because his doctors had deemed him too ill to go out.

His mind returned to little Ricky Lynch in the PICU. How small and fragile and vulnerable he'd looked. Thad's chest felt oddly hollow and cold. He remembered all too well having those feelings himself when he'd been in the hospital for the umpteenth time, and he never wanted to feel that vulnerable again.

He forced himself to focus on something else. The plans for the carnival, the things he needed to do for that. What he needed to talk to Emma about when she arrived here in a few minutes.

Emma.

With his past and his trust issues, Thad didn't do long-term relationships. He had needs, like everyone else. And those needs for intimacy were taken care of through short, carefully arranged affairs where both parties knew the rules and no deep emotions were involved. Afterward, they parted ways, both satisfied physically and with no ties or bad feelings emotionally. Not exactly fairy tale stuff, but it worked for him.

Or it had, until Emma arrived.

It was still hard to wrap his brain around their kiss. If it wasn't for the fact that his fingers still tingled with awareness from where he'd tangled them in her hair, or how when he licked his lips he swore he still tasted her there, he'd have denied it ever happened.

Most unsettling, though, had been the way she'd looked at him afterward. Like she'd seen him for the first time. Really seen him. And understood him. It was scary, being revealed like that, and Thad just didn't know what to do about it.

Part of him felt like maybe it was more about his return to the PICU and the emotions that always ran high when sick children were involved. He hadn't been there in years, doing his best to sequester the painful past away. But having Emma there with him today seemed to have widened fractures in the already-crumbling stone encasing his heart. Trouble was, he wasn't sure how to close the newly developed crack in his otherwise impenetrable armor.

With a sigh, he abandoned the window and walked over to sit in front of the crackling fire in the fireplace instead. Thad pulled up the app on his phone to check his blood sugar again, thinking perhaps his strange maudlin mood might have something to do with that. Ever since the episode in his kitchen, his blood sugar had fluctuated a lot and the exhaustion drove him nuts. He had things to do. Procedures to perfect. He couldn't sleep all day. For a man who'd always been up early and awake until the wee hours at night, it was unacceptable. In the past, once he'd gotten his insulin and eating schedule back on track things regulated quickly, but so far his diabetes was kicking his butt. Maybe he was getting old. Thirty-six was hardly ancient, but perhaps his underlying health condition was taking its toll.

In his mind his father's voice reverberated from beyond the grave.

Nothing but a sickly waste of space. Weakling. Good for nothing.

Thad scrubbed a hand over his face and shoved those hurtful memories aside. Ever. The awful man had died of a heart attack in South America five years ago, running away from his crimes to the end. He'd managed to avoid arrest, but hopefully had been punished just the same. Never putting down roots, always looking over his shoulder. Regardless, the man was no longer allowed to take up precious real estate in Thad's mind, though when he was tired or stressed, it was easier said than done.

In the corner of the study sat several large boxes marked Christmas Decorations on the sides in his mother's handwriting. His heart twisted again. He'd asked Everett to bring them down from the attic, thinking perhaps they could use something in there for the carnival, but it seemed rather silly now.

"Sir," his butler said from the doorway, as if conjured from Thad's thoughts. "Ms. Trudeau is here to see you."

"Thanks," Thad said, sighing. She'd texted him earlier that she had the day off and suggested they meet about the carnival plans. "Send her in."

Emma entered a few moments later, her braids loose once more as she walked across the huge Persian rug to sit in the chair opposite Thad's. Today she wore a pair of figure-hugging jeans that drew his gaze like a magnet to the sway of her hips. He looked back at the fire, forcing his attention from her pink lips and the memory of how soft and sweet they'd felt beneath his.

God, what's wrong with me?

"So," she said, clasping her hands atop the folder in her lap and breaking him out of his inappropriate erotic thoughts. "After meeting with Ricky on Wednesday, I think we need to take into account his wishes for the carnival."

Thad shifted in his seat slightly. "We are not having pony rides. The poop alone would be too much to deal with."

"No. Not ponies. I agree." She chuckled and shook her head. "Don't want to go there. But we need to nail down a location soon, so I can let the vendors know the space they'll have to work with. Also, seeing how fragile Ricky is only confirms for me that we need to keep it indoors and smaller, so these sick kids won't have issues getting around. Has your foundation had any luck securing a place?"

"Not yet. They contacted several places, but so far nothing's a done deal," he said, glad for a topic that didn't involve anything related to kissing. He told her about several spots around the city the Markson Foundation was looking at for the carnival and Emma took notes accordingly. Then awkward silence fell as he ran out of things to say.

She nodded and closed her folder, then tucked some braids behind her ear. Thad's fingertips itched, remembering how soft they'd felt against his skin. He had the crazy urge to slide his hands through them again, draw her near and kiss her until they were both breathless. Instead, he clenched his fists at his sides on the leather seat.

"How've you been feeling?" she asked at last, fiddling with the small sparkling stud earring in her earlobe. "After what happened in your kitchen the other night. Are you back on your schedule again? I'd hate to see you have another attack like that again."

He imagined running his tongue along that sensitive spot where her neck met her ear, feeling her shiver beneath him, moaning his name and…

Oh God. Stop thinking about that.

His throat constricted, making speech difficult. "I'm fine," Thad managed to squeak out, several octaves higher than usual. Restless and shaken by his emotional response to a woman he'd known such a short time, he pushed to his feet and paced the room. Not to mention the fact that he hated being fawned over. "Stop worrying about me."

"I'm a nurse. It's my job to worry about patients," she said, crossing her arms and forcing her breasts higher beneath her bright red turtleneck like she was presenting them to him as a gift.

Don't. Do not look at them.

Except now that was all Thad could seem to focus on. "Not that you're my patient," she went on quickly. "That would be weird. But I still feel responsible because I was there when it happened, and I care about you…" Her voice trailed off. "Because of the project, I mean."

I care about you…

There were times in Thad's past when he would've given up everything to hear those words from someone other than Everett. But part of the reason why he'd built such strong barriers around himself was so he didn't need them. Now, with Emma right here, offering him his innermost secret wish, Thad found himself completely flummoxed.

He turned away fast and stalked back to the window, away from temptation and yearning and the deep, aching, embarrassing need blossoming inside him, his face burning like the sun. He'd survived this long through sheer fractiousness and he couldn't turn his back on that now, not with Emma threatening all his long-held beliefs about himself and the world and everything he thought he had to be. It was too much, too soon and way too terrifying.

Thad turned back to face her; his tone harsh from desperation. "We're here to talk about the carnival, so let's stick to that, please."

Her dark eyes flashed fire for a second and Thad thought she'd argue with him about his abrupt change in topic. She moved closer and his pulse stumbled. If she touched him again now, all would be lost. He'd crumple like wet paper in her hands and tear apart just as easily. But she didn't touch him. Just stood a feet away, looking at him like she saw right through his BS and knew he was being a coward instead of facing up to what was happening between them. "Fine. Let's work."

* * *

After an hour and a half of planning and co-ordination, they took a break so Thad could check his blood sugar and give himself a small shot of insulin. Once he'd put everything away, he looked up at her from behind his desk while Emma studied the books on his shelves. It was an interesting assortment of everything from nonfiction to mysteries and thrillers to the odd women's fiction and romance story.

"You must read a lot, huh?" she asked him, eager to steer clear of the tension from before. This could be an interest they shared. "I love books. My mom used to read to me a lot as a kid and it stuck. When I was a teenager and we started reading the same stuff, we used to talk about them after, like our own little book club." Emma stopped, clearing her throat from the lump of sadness there. "Well, until she died, anyway."

God, this man made her so nervous. Why? Thad shouldn't make her heart race or her blood pound in her veins. And yes, they'd kissed back at the hospital, but that had been a mistake. A horrible, inexplicable mistake, completely not what she wanted at all.

Right?

Her uncertainty was even more unsettling.

Because maybe, just maybe, if she was honest with herself, she kind of had wanted to kiss Thad Markson. Maybe still wanted to kiss him now, despite him sending off clear don't-touch-me vibes. There was something so endearing, so intoxicatingly broken in him that called to the healer in her. The fact that he'd let her into his inner world that day in the PICU showed her he wasn't beyond redemption, no matter what he might try to portray to the others.

No. Emma knew in her heart the real Thad was still in there somewhere, the sad, sick, scared little boy he'd been before the death of his mother and his monster of a father had gotten to him. She wanted to help him find his way back to that boy again, if he'd let her.

But from the way Thad was avoiding the whole subject now, though, it was obviously not the time. He wasn't comfortable at present and neither was she. Best to focus on the project for now and get on with their planning. They could revisit the kiss and where they wanted things to go later, if they wanted. Time to change the subject. She looked over at the boxes in the corner and grinned. "Are you getting ready to decorate?"

"Huh?" Thad looked up from his laptop and frowned before tracking her gaze to the corner. "Oh, that." He gave a dismissive wave. "I had Everett bring those down from the attic earlier thinking we might be able to use them at the carnival, but it was a bad idea. He'll take them back up shortly."

"Why? Have you looked in them? Maybe there is something we could use." She got up and went over to peek inside the boxes. There was everything here—a tree, ornaments, garlands, wreaths, everything to make a home festive. Probably not the best choices for their carnival, he was right there, but why not use them anyway here? "I bet this place would look lovely all done up for the holidays. How about if we take a break and put up this stuff here in your office? I'll help. We could get this all unpacked and up in no time."

"Oh, I don't—" Thad started, but Emma already had part of the artificial tree out and on its stand where she started fluffing out the lower branches.

"Come on. It'll be fun," she said, grinning over at him behind the desk. And for the first time since their kiss, if felt like her nerves disappeared. "I promise."

For a moment Thad stared at her, then finally shook his head and joined her, grumbling under his breath about silly traditions and ridiculous extravagance as they got the rest of the tree up. It was bigger than she expected—at least eight feet tall—and moving into the spot he wanted in the corner was awkward, too, forcing them both to work together to avoid being buried under a mass of prickly fake pine.

Finally, with one last shove, Thad straightened, his high cheekbones flushed from the effort. "There. Satisfied?"

The tree stood to one side of the fireplace, a bit crooked, but they'd fix that in time.

"Not yet. But I will be." She winked at him, then began opening more boxes from the stack, pulling out swags of red, green and gold garlands. "We can use these on the tree and whatever's left over we can drape across the fireplace mantel. It will look beautiful."

Thad scowled as he pulled out handfuls of lights and gold stars and glittering berries from yet another box. "This is my private office, not the North Pole. I don't want anything to be garish or silly."

"Why not? It's Christmas. Everything is garish and loud and overblown this time of year. That's the joy of it." Thad gave her a look, then started throwing the lights on the tree haphazardly, with big wads of tangles everywhere. "No, no. That's not right." She pulled them off, then handed him the cord. "You need to plug them in first to make sure they work. Haven't you ever decorated a tree before?"

He hesitated for a second. "Not since my mother was alive."

Damn. Her heart squeezed. She should have connected those dots better. But now that she'd stepped in it, she needed to clean up her mess. Emma cleared her throat and tried again. "Well, then. I think it's time we started a new tradition ourselves, huh?"

Thad shrugged, then walked over to plug in the lights. They flickered at first, then glowed a warm gold color, twinkling off the silver star and berry ornaments piled on the floor beside them.

"Wow. These are beautiful. Leave them on while we decorate." Emma strung the lights around the tree. "Did both of your parents work?"

"Only my father. Too much." He fed her more lights, pointing out empty spots as she worked. "My mother was on the board of several charities in the city, but mainly she stayed home, with me. At least until she got sick."

His voice trailed off and Emma looked down at him from where she'd climbed the ladder to reach the top of the tree. "That must've been so hard for you, losing her support."

"It was," he said, moving in behind her at the bottom of the ladder to steady it, essentially caging her in while continuing to feed more string lights to her and making sure she didn't fall. If Emma didn't know better, she'd think they'd landed in one of those cheesy TV holiday movies where she falls and ends up his arms, sharing a first kiss under the mistletoe.

Or another kiss. Because she and Thad had already kissed behind a Christmas tree.

And it had been nice. More than nice. Sweet and warm and seductive and...

"Here." He handed her the rest of the lights in the bundle. "I'll grab another from the box."

Emma turned back toward the tree, feeling a bit shaky. This was no movie and Thad Markson was not her romantic hero, even if he did have that whole broody, gorgeous grump thing going for him.

Do not go there. Emma repeated to herself, like maybe it would stick. *This is for Ricky. Not you. Don't screw up your chance at a promotion over a man. People leave. People die. Be responsible.*

The ladder wobbled a bit as Thad climbed up behind her and his weight settled on the wood. "These are multicolored." He held out another string of lights to her, his body so close to hers now she could feel the heat of him through her clothes and smell his woodsy, clean aftershave. "Not ideal since they don't match the others, but they're all that's left in the box."

"Uh…" Emma made the mistake of looking back at him over her shoulder and, oh, boy. His face was right there, near enough to kiss him again, if she wanted. And man, did she want. Except no. They weren't doing that again. Not now. Maybe not ever. To distract herself from the need now churning through her system, Emma grabbed the lights from him and weaved them in with the others, inching closer to the top of the tree. Each time she moved up a rung, Thad did the same behind her, increasing the sizzling tension between them that apparently only she could feel because Thad continued scowling at the lights like they held all of his attention.

Once they finally got the entire tree lit, Thad stepped down off the ladder, followed by Emma. She stepped back to admire their handiwork and accidentally brushed against his chest with her shoulder.

"Sorry." She moved away, doing her best to concentrate on the task at hand and not the hunky surgeon beside her as she picked up another box full of gorgeous red and gold glass ornaments. The mesmerizing iridescent sheen on them showed their quality and cost. Probably handmade. Way out of her price range to be sure, but they reminded her of the old hand-me-down ornaments her parents had used every year. Same magical feel, way less expensive. The lower cost never affected their beauty. "These are amazing. I've never seen decorations like this before."

"My mother bought them from a Bavarian market one year," he said, holding one up in front of him so the lights from the tree cast rainbow shards around the room. "They were her pride and joy."

The sudden tenderness in his voice had Emma blinking hard against the unexpected sting of tears. The last thing she wanted to do today was start crying in front of Thad, so instead, she gestured toward the tree. "Since all this was your mother's, I think you should have the honor of placing the first ornament."

"Oh, I..." Thad frowned, as if only then realizing she was still there. "Let's do it together."

She took a deep breath, her heart pinching

again. "But it's obvious this meant so much to your mother and..."

He continued watching her, waiting.

"Fine. It's making me sad, okay?" She threw up her hands, exasperated. "You're not the only one with fond memories of your long-lost parents. All this reminds me of when my mom and dad used to decorate the tree with me and Karley. The holidays are hard for everyone. Doesn't mean we still shouldn't celebrate them."

Saying it out loud seemed to open the floodgates of her past, causing a tidal wave of memories to rush back to her, just as vivid and real as the day they'd happened. The scent of the pine incense her dad used to light. The jolly sounds of Christmas carols on the radio. The sweetness of the cookies and eggnog they set out for Santa. Bittersweet now, all of it. Emma had tried hard to re-create those memories for Karley after their parents were gone, but it never felt quite the same.

Thad, thankfully, seemed to realize she needed some space, because he stopped questioning her and began decorating the tree alone. She held the box and handed him the ornaments while he hung them. Like clockwork they went, making a good team—same as they'd done in the ER—until the last box was empty. They stood shoulder to shoulder across the room then, admiring their work. Magical.

Soon though, the mood in the room changed. Thad's arm bumped Emma's, sending fresh waves of awareness through her nerve endings.

"My father wasn't around very much after my mother died. Which was good, since he hated me."

Stunned, Emma glanced up at him, noticing for the first time the row of tiny freckles covering the bridge of his nose. "I'm sure that's not true. No parent hates their own child."

"He did." Thad stared straight ahead at the tree, his voice low and devoid of emotion. "He never missed an opportunity to tell me what a disappointment I was to him. How my disease made me weak and defective. How he wished I'd never been born. It's those words that spur me on today. The burning desire to prove to him that he was wrong. In so many ways."

Something clicked for her then. That's why he acted the way he did, keeping everyone away. Not because he was truly a Grinch, but because of what had happened to him growing up. "You aren't, you know," she said, watching his throat work as he swallowed hard. "Defective or weak. You aren't a disappointment at all, Thad. You have nothing to prove to anyone."

"Hmm." He continued staring at the tree. "Perhaps. But you don't forget those scars. Not ever."

A red and gold glow bathed the room now, lending a new warmth and intimacy to the space. Emma felt like the final walls between them had crashed down and for the first time she saw the real Thad. The one she'd suspected lurked beneath his grouchy exterior the whole time.

"I remember being in the PICU after my mom died," Thad continued, his voice monotone as more painful memories surfaced. Emma didn't interrupt, knowing he needed to get this out to help him heal. "He told them to keep me. That he didn't want me around until I was normal again." A tiny muscle near his jaw worked. "I knew, even then, that it had to be the grief talking. He was upset about my mother dying. I loved him. He was my father. I didn't want to think the worst. But even after they got my blood sugar stabilized and I came home, nothing changed. Well, except my father. All he cared about from that point forward was his work. He became obsessed with money. Making it, spending it. His wealth consumed him. And when he was threatened with the loss of that wealth, he took whatever means necessary to keep it—even if it meant hurting and cheating other people to do it. If he hadn't died from a heart attack when he did, I fully believe he would've been investigated by the SEC and found guilty. As it was, he died and left me with a mess and a scandal to clean up. I did both. And I've never taken a cent of his dirty money. All of it went to his victims and to the foundation to help other people and do good in the world. Even this town house is owned by the foundation. When I die, they have instructions to donate it to the city to be used as a museum or school or whatever else they need. His was a legacy of pain. I refuse to continue it onward. The pain stops with me."

"Oh, Thad," she whispered again, not knowing what else to say, her own heart breaking for him. Without thinking, she entwined her fingers with his and he let her. "You've been through so much and deserved none of it. But what you're doing now, it's so good. You'll make a difference to so many people."

He still wasn't looking at her, but she saw the sheen in his eyes. "The only person who was ever there for me after my mom died was Everett. He sat with me, helped me with my homework, played with me. He's more of a father to me than my own ever was."

She'd sensed there was more of a relationship between the two men than employer and employee from the first night she'd come here, but now it made so much sense. "I'm glad he was there for you, Thad. Every child needs someone to care for them. I've tried to step in and be that for Karley, too." Emma sighed. "Not sure I've done enough, though. Weird, but it's easier taking care of other people as a nurse than it is those closest to you sometimes."

Thad finally looked at her. "I haven't met your sister, Emma, but I bet you've done a wonderful job. You're one of the kindest people I've ever met."

"Thank you. I appreciate you saying that."

He put his arm around her shoulders—a bit stiffly, as if he wasn't used to showing affection—and drew her into his side. Emma didn't move at first, stunned, then slowly shifted to face him. Most people

feared Thad, but not Emma. Never again.
Not after tonight.

The flames in the fireplace crackled and
shadows played in the glow from the tree,
making the moment seem moody, mysteri-
ous and infinitely romantic. She licked her
lips and he tracked the tiny movement with
his gaze. Her breath caught as he dipped
his head, thinking he was going to kiss her
again. But then his cheek brushed hers as he
buried his face in her hair and inhaled deep.

"I'm glad you're here, Emma," Thad said,
his voice deep and rough.

"Me, too." The words didn't come out
as firm as Emma wanted because just then
Thad's lips trailed around her ear, moving
slowly across her cheekbone and down to her
mouth. This time was different from their
sweet kiss in the PICU lobby. Now it felt hot
and needy, enough to rock her world like a
shaken-up snow globe. Thad held her tight
to him, as if afraid she'd disappear. After
what he'd been through as a kid, maybe he
was. Emma wanted to heal his wounds, make
his holidays warm and bright and happy for
once. She slid her hand from his chest, the
soft hair at the nape of his neck tickling her
fingertips, urging her to sink into him even
more…

It took her a moment then to process the cold rush of air between them. He returned to the window, alone. Her lips tingled and her head felt stuffy with emotions. She hugged her arms around herself against a shudder. "Thad, I…"

"I think you should go," he said, still staring outside, his breath fogging the glass. "Have Everett get your things and call you a taxi home. I'll pay for it."

"But…" she whispered, still feeling a bit dazed.

Thad stalked toward the office door then, his words a rush as he passed her. "My foundation is setting up a holiday fundraiser for the end of next week for all of the charities we support, including the wish project. I'd like you to accompany me to the event."

She blinked at him, still trying to process his abrupt change in mood, let alone his words. "I, uh…"

"I'll text you the exact date and time," he said to her, stopping on the threshold of the doorway to glance back at her. "It will be formal, so I'll have one of the local stores send something to your apartment for you to wear to the event. Just give Everett your sizes and he'll arrange everything else. Good night, Emma."

He walked out, leaving her to stare after him, wondering when exactly she'd become Cinderella in their crazy Christmas fairy tale.

CHAPTER SEVEN

"Wow!" Karley said when Emma came out of her bedroom the following Friday evening, dressed in the figure-hugging, scarlet, off-the-shoulder, below-the-knee cocktail dress one of the fancy designer boutiques on Fifth Avenue had sent over earlier, per Thad's promised orders. And it wasn't just the dress, either. There'd been shoes and jewelry and even a small beaded handbag to go with it.

Part of her wondered exactly what kind of game he was playing—and if she was bold enough to go along with it. They hadn't really spoken much since the kiss at his place, other than quick texts and calls about the carnival, so she had no clue where any of this was going. She'd thought about canceling, but no. Tonight was important for the carnival, so she needed to be there.

And another part of her told her to just enjoy the ride. She worked hard. She deserved some fun. And really, it was all just fun, right? This thing between them couldn't actually go anywhere long-term. Their lives were too different. They wanted different things. She loved her independence too much.

Emma did a little spin on her red high heels and grinned at her reflection in the mirror. Okay. Fine. She did feel like she'd been visited by a fairy godmother this afternoon, instead of just the normal delivery guy. And damn if she didn't like it. Probably more than she should.

After a final adjustment to her dress, she stepped out into the living room and cleared her throat to get her sister's attention. "So, you like it? You don't think I look silly all fancied up this way?"

"*Silly* is the last word I'd use to describe you, sis." Karley looked up from where she sat on the sofa, watching TV and typing on her phone, her expression suitably impressed. "Wow! You look like you're ready for the red carpet or something."

"Thanks." Emma blushed and smoothed a hand over the silky fabric of her gown. She'd never worn a garment so expensive in her life and she rarely had a chance to dress up these days, so tonight was special. And important. In more ways than one. She knew it was important to convince the donors to give money at the fundraiser and she needed to look the part of a wealthy, successful project coordinator in order to do that. But part of her also secretly hoped Thad liked how she looked, too.

They'd only texted each other since the night in his office when they'd put up the decorations and then... Lord help her, Emma's whole body still tingled at the thought of their steamy second kiss.

It had been good. *Really* good.

Then things had cooled off fast between them.

At first, she'd been hurt. But then she'd remembered what he'd told her about himself and his past, and she understood why he was hesitant. She wasn't ready to jump into anything either, to be truthful. She'd dated before, off and on, and been with other men. Nothing serious, though. Emma was too focused on her career and building a life for herself and her sister to go all gaga over some man. Then along came Thad Markson, and for some odd reason, he'd ticked her boxes. Gotten around her barriers and laid her vulnerabilities bare. At first glance he wasn't the type she usually went for—funny, kind, outgoing. But his brokenness called to the healer in her. The very brusqueness and broodiness that drove others away drew her like a moth to a flame. Maybe because she'd suffered great loss early in life, too. Maybe because she knew what it was like to forge ahead alone, making up for what you lacked. And maybe it was just the fact that deep down she knew he hurt and she wanted to let him know he wasn't alone...

"Ready to wheel and deal for your charity event?" Karley asked, breaking into her thoughts.

"I think so." Emma shook off the pensiveness that had settled over her as she'd thought about her complicated relationship with Thad and walked over to sit on the opposite end of the sofa to wait for the driver to arrive. "I'm not really a big schmoozer, but if it means being able to grant Ricky's wish, I'll try." She checked her watch. "Are you set for dinner? Okay here by yourself for a couple hours?"

"I'm fine, sis." Karley managed not to roll her eyes at Emma, though it was implied in her tone. "Stop worrying about me, Em. I'll be eighteen in a few months, the same age you were when Mom and Dad died. Practically an adult. By this time next year, I'll be away at college and doing my own thing."

"Don't remind me."

"So." Her sister shifted slightly on the cushion to face Emma, tucking one leg beneath her. "You like this guy, huh?"

"What? No." Emma did her best to hide her smile and failed miserably. "We're just partners on this project, that's all."

"Uh-huh. Sure." Karley sounded completely unconvinced. "Well, whatever it is, I'm happy for you. Haven't seen you glow this much in a long time."

"I'm not glowing!" Emma looked up sharply, her cheeks prickling with shock. "Am I?"

"Oh, yeah. Definitely glow happening there." Karley gestured toward Emma and grinned. "You deserve it, sis. Go for it."

Before Emma could say anything else, a knock sounded on their apartment door. Damn. Her driver. She took a deep breath and stood, still not sure how she felt about her attraction to Thad being so obvious to everyone. "I need to go," she said, pulling her coat from the closet and slipping it on. "I'll be back by eleven."

"Don't hurry on my account," Karley said as Emma grabbed her tiny evening bag and opened the door. "Have fun!"

"I'll try." She started out into the hallway

with the driver, then said over her shoulder. "Be good!"

"Be better!" Karley shouted back. It was kind of their ritual.

She followed the driver downstairs and thanked him for holding the back door of the black limo open for her. Emma climbed inside and looked over to see Thad across from her, looking like he'd stepped right out of a high-fashion modeling shoot in his tailored tux and crisp white shirt. Then the driver closed the door, and the overhead light went out, leaving them in sudden darkness.

"Good evening, Emma," he said from the shadows. "You look lovely. I knew that color would suit you well."

"You picked this out yourself?" she asked as the limo pulled away from the curb and merged into traffic. "I thought you had surgeries booked all week."

"I did." He turned to look out the window beside him at the passing Christmas lights. "But I gave the personal shopper strict instructions on what I wanted and your sizes. It looks like she did an excellent job."

"Thank you for all this," Emma said, clutching her tiny bag like a shield in her lap. "It's very generous of you."

"It's necessary to make a good impression on the people we'll meet tonight." They stopped at a light, and he looked over at her again, those icy eyes of his skimming over her like a physical touch. A shudder of awareness went through her before she could stop it. Emma hugged her coat tighter around herself. "Not that you aren't beautiful the way you usually are. It's just I find presenting a certain image acts as additional armor."

I know. Emma bit back those words and swallowed them down. Thad exuded a low-key disdain to keep others at bay. It worked a lot of the time, too. Except with her, because she saw through it. *Armor* was a good word to describe Thad's attitude. Push others away before they did the same to you. The fact that Emma was here tonight felt even more special, taken in that light.

"Well, I appreciate you thinking of me."

"I always think of you these days, Emma."

Oh boy. Her chest tightened at his quiet words; she was thankful he couldn't see her face because it had to be as red as her dress now. He couldn't mean… Unless he did. Had he been thinking about their kisses as much as Emma had? Imagining what might have happened if they hadn't stopped there? If he'd led her up to his bedroom and locked the door and…

Inside she flailed with want, struggling to keep her breath calm.

As they rode through blue-collar Queens, Thad glanced at the passing scenery. "So, this is your neighborhood?"

"Yes." Emma smiled, grateful for the mundane topic. "Long way from your Fifth Avenue town house, but we like it."

"We?"

"My sister and I."

"Right," he said, frowning at her. "Karley. How old is she again?"

"Seventeen, going on thirty." Emma's grinned with pride. "She's great. Straight-A student. Working toward a full scholarship to Howard University after she graduates."

"That's impressive." Thad shifted a bit in his seat, light filtering in through the window illuminated the front of his tux jacket, reminding her again of his broad shoulders and tight torso. "What does she want to study in college?"

"Premed," Emma said. "God help her."

Thad chuckled. "It's challenging, no lie. But worth it if it's the right fit for you."

"I think it is, for her." She met his gaze. "But no matter what she wanted to do, I'd support her."

"I'm sure you would."

The ride to the small event center was quiet after that, Emma's stomach filling with nervous butterflies. Not so much because of the fundraiser, but because of the man across from her. She kept reminding herself that this was not a date. Though, wow. It really did feel like one.

Once they arrived, the driver held the door for Thad, then he came around himself to help Emma out. He took her hand and kept hold of it, his grip firm and warm. Comforting. After making their way inside and checking their coats at the booth near the entrance, they walked into a banquet room decorated like a winter wonderland. White linen tablecloths, huge bouquets of white roses and lilies and paperwhites adorning the center of each table. From the sparkling champagne flutes and real silverware to the dangling lights and iridescent streamers, the entire place screamed wealth. There was even a small string quartet in one corner playing live Christmas music. Emma hesitated on the threshold, taking it all in. Despite her wishes, it really did feel like a fairy tale.

"Everything okay?" Thad asked near her ear, his expression concerned. "You look a bit flushed."

Any warmth now was because of the tickle

of his breath on her cheek, the brush of his body against hers as they walked, the reassuring squeeze of his fingers. She had it bad for him, and that wasn't good.

Stop. Enjoy tonight for what it is.

She took a deep breath, then smiled. "I'm good. There are so many people here."

"Yes." Thad winked. "But you're the only one here with me."

Those words surrounded her like a fuzzy blanket as they entered the room and Thad introduced her to person after person, enough to make her head swim after a while. So many of the city's powerful and elite. Given what he'd told her about his family and his father's scandals, Emma knew what a big deal it was for Thad to be here tonight, and she wanted to support him in any way she could, so she stayed by his side. He put on a good show of being above it all, but still. It seemed everyone wanted to greet him, talk to him, be around him. Everyone carefully avoiding the subject of Thad's father, she noticed, which Emma was grateful for. Thad even managed to get several of the guests to commit to sizable donations to their charity project.

They got a short break during dinner, where they were partially hidden from the others at their table by the large centerpiece and out of the immediate spotlight. She glanced over at Thad then and noticed the tightness at the corners of his mouth and eyes he couldn't hide, showing the toll being here had taken on him. Emma placed her hand over his chilled one on the table and squeezed. He was picking at their delicious chicken and roasted veggies. From the artful arrangement of the food on the plate, she was sure it was gourmet expensive, but she'd have been just as happy with a burger and fries.

"Here," she said, picking up a nearby basket of fancy whole-grain artisan rolls. "Eat one of these. You should, to keep your sugar balanced. And have some water. You look stressed."

"I'm fine." He shook his head and exhaled slowly. "I'm just looking forward to leaving."

"I understand." She squeezed his hand again. "And thank you."

"For what?"

"For being here tonight. Hopefully, we'll raise all the funds to make Ricky's wish come true."

"We will. I'll make sure of it."

After the delicious dinner the quartet played several holiday-themed ballads, and couples moved around the dance floor set up in one corner. Emma watched them sway to the music while Thad chatted up yet another donor. She lost herself in the beauty of the music until Thad held out his hand.

"Care to dance?"

"Oh." She blinked at him a moment, her heart tripping over itself. "I don't think…"

Not a date. Not a date. Not a date.

"I do," he said, taking her hand and leading her toward the dance floor. And damn if she didn't feel like a princess being led by her Prince Charming. Or Grinch Charming in this case. Though it was getting harder and harder to associate Thad with that green cartoon figure.

Thad took her in his arms just as the band started playing a rendition of the waltz from *Anastasia*. Even with her high heels, she had to look up at him.

"Have I mentioned how beautiful you look tonight?" he asked, his gaze skimming over her. "Because you do, Emma. You really do. Scrubs don't do you justice."

"Yes, you have. And thank you, Thad." They continued around the floor, him deftly steering them around the other couples around them. Emma was impressed. "You're a good dancer."

"My mother gave me lessons when I was

young. It's like riding a bike." Thad glanced down at her and almost smiled before admitting, "One of those things you don't really forget."

Eventually the music changed to her bittersweet favorite, "Have Yourself a Merry Little Christmas." With a contented sigh, she laid her cheek against Thad's chest, soaking in the magic of the evening.

They swayed together, bodies brushing, his heat melting her like a marshmallow in hot cocoa.

"You always smell so good," he said, nuzzling the top of her head. "Like cinnamon and roses."

She grinned, murmuring against his tux lapel, "You smell good, too."

From the corner of her eye, she spotted several of the people they'd talked with earlier watching them with curiosity. Emma straightened.

Thad frowned down at her. "What?"

"We should be careful," she said, glancing around. "Everyone will think we're a couple."

He stilled, scowling. "I don't do couples, Emma."

Despite knowing this wasn't a date or anything serious, her stomach still sank with disappointment. "I didn't say we were one. Just that people might think that."

It was silly to be hurt by his words. Emma knew that. She had no right getting upset over something that was never meant to be in the first place, regardless of the fairy-tale setting. Still, her heart ached and her temples throbbed. Fine. Maybe she'd let herself believe there was the possibility of something between her and Thad after they'd kissed. Anybody would, right? But she wasn't a fool. She didn't belong in his world of glittering banquets and fancy houses and expensive clothes. She was just a normal woman with a normal life. If Thad wasn't interested in that, in her, she wouldn't try to convince him otherwise. He could take her or leave her. She didn't need to change for a man. She had plenty going on in her life without him. She was more than fine with who she was.

Emma stepped out of his arms and crossed her own. "We should probably go. It's getting late."

He studied her, clearly confused. "I'm not sure what's happening here."

"Neither am I. And that's the problem." She walked back toward their table, eyes prickling. She refused to cry. Emma never cried. Not since the day of her parents' funeral. Thad followed behind her, his heat at her back a constant reminder of what she couldn't have, shouldn't have, but wanted desperately anyway.

They said their goodbyes and thanked the people who had donated to Ricky's cause, then went to get their coats. Thad helped Emma into hers, then kept his hands on her shoulders, taking a deep breath. "You're right."

Now she was confused, frowning up at him over her shoulder. "About what?"

"Us. This. Whatever it is." He gave a vague wave between them before walking her out to their limo parked at the curb once more. Thad held the door for her, then climbed inside to sit across from her again. "We came here tonight to fundraise, but…" He huffed out a breath, then stared out the window next to him as they drove through the New York night. "I don't know. Something's changed."

"How?" Emma asked, feeling like if they didn't get it out now, they never would.

Thad shook his head, still staring out the window beside him at the crowds gathered at Rockefeller Center's ice rink. "I can't stop thinking about you, Emma. About that kiss in my study."

The butterflies inside her swarmed and her

throat constricted, making words difficult. But she managed to whisper the truth burning a hole inside her. "Me neither."

He moved then, sitting beside her, the length of his body pressed against hers, the sound of his breath as ragged as her pulse. "I want you, Emma. I haven't stopped wanting you since the night in my office. Seeing you now, looking so beautiful and holding you as we danced. I know we shouldn't, because I meant what I said about relationships. I'm not good at them and I don't do them."

The pain in his voice overshadowed any sting in his words. He was broken inside. Broken and beautiful and so beyond anything she'd ever experienced before, she was completely hooked. Emma didn't need a cheesy holiday film ending, she realized. She just needed Thad. More than she'd needed anyone in a long, long time.

She cupped his cheek, forcing him to meet her gaze. "What do you want?"

"Emma," he whispered against her forehead, his jaw flexing beneath her palm. Thad pulled back to meet her gaze, icy eyes flashing fire, possessive and primal and potent.

She slipped her other hand around his neck, toying with the soft hair at his nape, twirling the silky dark strands around her finger. "I don't know what's happening here or how any of this will turn out, but I do know that I want to find out. With you."

For the hundredth time that week, Thad wondered what in the hell he was doing as Emma texted her sister to let her know she might be late and to not wait up and he let the driver know to head to his town house instead of Queens.

But it was so difficult to think rationally, to keep his cool, to push his emotions aside when Emma was this close to him. She was stunningly beautiful, soft and warm and giving. And she wanted him.

Throat tight, he focused on keeping some semblance of sanity in the back of that car despite the desperation to have her clawing inside him. This was no way to be together the first time—frantic and fumbling in the back seat where anyone could see them. No. If this was going to happen with Emma, he wanted it to be perfect.

So he needed to keep his mind off the sweet scent of her washing over him in the tight confines of the limo. Speaking of tight, his pants were becoming increasingly uncomfortable as they constrained a certain part of his anatomy responding directly to the press of Emma's thigh against the side of his. Not helpful. What also wasn't helpful was how each time he closed his eyes, he pictured Emma gazing up at him as they'd danced, looking at him like she saw only the good, the right, the admirable in him. Worse, it made him yearn to be that man for her. Like it was that easy.

And maybe he would be with her by his side.

But no. There'd be no sides, no support, because this would only be a one-night affair. That was all it could ever be.

Right?

Right. Because Emma deserved better than him. If she stayed by his side, Thad feared his father had been right. That he was truly worthless and weak and he'd drain all the good right out of whatever this was between them. Not on purpose; things happened. They always did with him. She'd told him people called him a Grinch at the hospital, and they were probably right. He lived alone—except for Everett and Baxter—he rarely let anyone close to him for a reason. He'd become used to the self-imposed isolation.

At least until Emma had arrived.

Now Thad wasn't so sure. About anything.

"Done," Emma said, slipping her phone back into her impossibly tiny purse, then kissing his cheek. "Karley's alerted and has secured herself in the apartment for the night."

Thad then took a deep breath, wondering if the adrenaline racing through his veins like Santa's reindeer was a sign of excitement or caution. Ten minutes later they pulled up to the curb on Fifth Avenue and the driver opened Thad's door for him, jarring him from his thoughts. "We've arrived, sir."

"Thank you." Thad climbed out and adjusted his topcoat, his heart slamming against his rib cage so hard he feared it might burst out onto the sidewalk. He was no virgin. He'd been with plenty of women in his time, but this thing with Emma felt different. Perhaps because he'd told her things about himself, his deepest, darkest secrets, and instead of running away or breaking his confidence, she'd accepted him. His chest squeezed tight with what that might mean, for him and for the future.

Thad walked around to open Emma's door and help her out of the vehicle. The same crackling chemistry between them flared hotter, and suddenly there was no more time to debate his actions. He needed Emma upstairs, in his bed. Now. They hurried inside, Thad bypassing Everett with a muttered word about his butler taking the rest of the night off, and Thad took her to his private suite on the top floor.

"Oh my!" Emma gaped at his luxurious surroundings as he shut and locked the door behind them. This room was his sanctuary, the place in the town house he spent the most time, other than his office on the third floor. He'd had it redecorated a few years earlier, with lots of darker colors and soothing fabrics. Everett had lit a fire, as usual, and turned down the white satin sheets on Thad's huge king-size poster bed. "This place is like a dream world." Her grin turned wicked, and his taut body tightened even more. "A fantasy."

Thad removed his coat and draped it over the back of a chair, then took Emma's as well and did the same with it. "I don't bring many people up here."

"I feel honored," she said, her tone teasing.

Thad wasn't a man who was teased often, but from Emma he loved it. Loved her wonderful, giving nature. In fact, the more time Thad spent with her, the more he craved. She was like a drug, and he was addicted, for better or worse.

Emma believed in the goodness of humanity. She gave of herself without asking for anything in return. The cruelty of Thad's father had taught him differently. But for a few shining moments, Emma made him feel better, less alone. Made him believe again. Even as she made him forget everything else but her.

And that's how he knew he should stay away. Because if he wasn't careful, he'd start believing those things as well and his armor would be gone. He couldn't allow that to happen. He feared it was already too late.

"Come here." He pulled her into his arms and kissed her, hoping to stem the tide of helplessness flooding his system. Control. He needed control here, even as the sweetness of her lips threatened to rob him of it. She gasped and he swept his tongue inside, tasting her as he slid his hands down her body, touching, caressing, claiming.

Instead of pulling away, though, Emma met him kiss for kiss, tangle for tangle, pressing against him, holding him tighter, as if she wanted to remember everything about him, too. She shoved his tux jacket off his shoulders, leaving it in a pile on the floor. Undid his bow tie and tossed it aside.

When they finally pulled back for breath, Thad whispered, "I want you so much."

She slid her leg up the outside of his thigh in answer, taking that red dress with it.

"God, Emma," Thad groaned. All that smooth flesh exposed for him made him crazy to touch it. He nuzzled her throat, nibbling down to the base of her neck. The heat of her scorched his lips, bringing the simmering need within him to a full boil. His steady surgeon's fingers fumbled for the zipper at the back of her dress, drawing it open as she growled low and buried her face in his throat, loving how responsive Emma was to his touch.

"Hurry." She wriggled against him as his hand slipped inside her dress to stroke her exposed back. "Please..."

"You like that?" He smiled against the side of her neck, then licked the raging pulse at the base of her throat. Emma shivered, her head thrown back, eyes closed in wild abandon. "Tell me what you want."

"You. I want you."

That's all Thad needed to hear. The red dress slid off Emma, pooling around her feet, and for a second, he just took in the sight of her in only her lingerie and heels. The image would be seared into his mind forever. He pulled her back into his arms to rain kisses on her shoulders. "You're perfect, Emma. The closest thing I'll ever find to heaven."

God, he couldn't remember ever wanting anyone else this much.

She took his hand and led him to the bed. "Lie down."

Thad did, swallowing hard when she climbed atop him to straddle him. Emma made quick work of his shirt, running her hands over his torso as if to memorize every inch of him. Then she kissed the middle of his chest, right over his thundering heart, and Thad melted like a snowman in a furnace.

He thought of facts, figures, medical journals. Anything to blunt his need, anything to make this last longer, because he wanted this to go all night. Wanted to kiss every inch of her.

But where Emma was concerned, he only had the time setting—now!

Ending her sweet torture, he rolled her beneath him and took charge, pinning her hands beside her head, enveloped in her legs around his waist, the heat between her thighs rocking against his hardness.

"I need you, Thad," she urged. "Please."

"I need you, too, Emma." More than he'd ever imagined possible. Rolling slightly to

his side, Thad quickly removed Emma's bra
and panties and his own pants and boxer
briefs, leaving them both naked, hot and
panting. His lips went to her breast, teasing
her nipple with his tongue, while her hand
slid down to close around his length, making
him shudder and groan. So good. He kissed
lower, making love to her with his lips and
tongue until she arched and cried out her
first release.

It was all too much. It would never be
enough.

When Thad could take no more, he rolled
away to grab a condom from his nightstand
drawer and put it on before stretching out
atop her once more. He rested his weight on
his forearms on either side of her head, his
gaze locked on her sated one, his tip poised
at her wet entrance. "Ready."

"So ready," she said, then pulled his mouth
to hers for another kiss.

Thad sank into her in one long thrust, sa-
voring the tight heat of her body around his.
Then he held still, allowing her to adjust to
him until she grew restless and demanded
more.

"You feel…" she said, gasping as he began
a slow, steady rhythm that had them both
careering toward ecstasy all too soon. Her

hands were on his back, stroking his skin in slow, rough caresses before she dug her nails into his butt, meeting him thrust for thrust. Thad felt like every nerve ending in his body was on fire, demanding release of a powerful, stormy, wild hunger that stole his breath.

Emma cried out again, riding the waves of her second climax and pushing Thad past the point of no return. Soon, he let go as well, throbbing with his own pleasure.

Eventually, they floated back down to earth, limp and tangled together in his big bed, his head on her chest, her fingers in his hair. Reluctantly, Thad got up to use the restroom, then returned to pull a limp, sated Emma into his side. She sighed and cuddled closer.

"That was…" She kissed the pulse point at the base of his throat. "Wow."

"Hmm." He closed his eyes, his head blissfully clear and blank for a while. "Agreed. When do you need to get home?"

"Soon," she whispered, kissing him again. "But not yet."

"Good." Thad smiled as he drifted to sleep. Eventually Everett would call her a cab and she'd go back to her life and he to his, but for now, Emma was here with him, and he wanted to enjoy it for as long as it lasted.

CHAPTER EIGHT

THE SOUND OF cold reality woke Thad early the next morning.

His cell phone.

With a groan he rolled over and stretched an arm out to grab his phone from the night-stand, painfully aware of the patch of cold mattress beside him where Emma had been earlier. He peeked open an eye and saw a hastily scrawled sticky note stuck on her pillow saying, "Thanks for last night. Call you later," followed by a string of *x*'s and *o*'s. His heart gave a little pinch and his lips twitched into a smile.

So sweet, my Emma.

Thad bolted up in bed, now fully awake, and not just because he was on call that day. Damn. When the hell had he begun having... *feelings*...for Emma? Beyond desire, beyond attraction. Beyond anything he'd felt for anyone in a long, long time and far more dangerous than he'd ever intended. Lo—

Buzz. Buzz. Buzz.

His phone kept him from finishing that last word, thank goodness. Because Thad Markson was not a man who fell head over heels. Oh no. He was far too precise and orderly and career-focused for that. And not even someone as kind and lovely and sexy and perfect as Emma Trudeau would change him.

Maybe she already has...

Dammit. His orderly universe had been rocked and for once in his life, he wanted to ignore the call, but couldn't. Duty called. Literally.

Scowling, he hit the answer button on the phone and tossed the covers aside, padding across the room to the attached master bath as he spoke. "Dr. Markson." The woman from the after-hours service gave him the rundown on the case as he raked his fingers through his disheveled hair and stared at his reflection in the mirror. "I'll be there in half an hour. Have them prep an OR and take the patient up."

He ended the call and hopped in the shower, then quickly shaved and dressed. The patient was one he'd seen in the ER the week before—an elderly woman named Lovelace. She'd returned to Manhattan West last night complaining of chest pain and sudden shortness of breath. They'd been running tests on her since, thinking it might be related to her heart failure, but Thad disagreed. Given the woman's history, he suspected a pulmonary embolism, which could be life-threatening if not handled quickly and properly. He exited his bedroom and called for Everett as he descended the stairs toward the kitchen. "I need to go in to the hospital. Emergency case. Can you have the driver meet me out front, please?"

"Certainly, sir," Everett said, already waiting for him with hot coffee, oatmeal with fresh berries, and an early edition of the financial newspaper on a tray for Thad. The older man set it all on the island's granite countertop, then turned to walk out of the kitchen.

That's when Thad noticed the slightly grayish pallor to his butler's complexion. Given it was predawn, it could be the early hour, but Thad was still concerned. His closest confidant wasn't a spring chicken anymore. "Everything all right, Everett? You look unwell today."

"Fine, sir. Fine," the older man said, waving off Thad's worry. "Bit of insomnia, that's all. I'll alert the driver of your impending departure."

Thad stared at the empty doorway a moment longer before turning his attention to his breakfast. His insulin pump and sensor were both waterproof, meaning he could wear them in the shower, which was great. But the hot water did cause his body to absorb his insulin more quickly, so it was important for him to keep his blood sugar regulated now. Plus, if he had to take the Lovelace patient into surgery, which he suspected he would, he may not have a chance to eat again for a while.

He quickly paged through the stock reports, but his focus was elsewhere. Mainly on Emma and the blissful night they'd spent together. It had been amazing, being with her like that. Their chemistry was off the charts, and they'd been so in sync, like two pieces of the same puzzle, almost knowing what the other needed before they said anything.

Baxter came up and nudged Thad's leg with his nose, tail wagging and tongue lolling. Thad smiled down at him and bent to scratch the dog behind his ears. "Hey, boy. Good morning to you, too."

"The car is ready for you, sir," Everett said, reappearing the doorway.

"Thank you." Thad finished the rest of his food and coffee fast, then stood. "I should be home for dinner tonight. Usual time."

"Very good, sir," Everett said, then turned away to cough.

"Are you sure you're all right?" Thad stopped next to the butler and put a hand on the older man's shoulder. "Do I need to examine you? Maybe you're coming down with something?"

"No, sir. Really," Everett said, holding up his hand. "It's just a cold. Nothing to worry about."

Thad watched his old friend closely for a moment, then nodded. "Call me if you change your mind."

"Yes, sir." The butler helped Thad into his coat, then held the door for him as he exited, waving from the top of the stoop. "Good day, sir."

Even early in the morning the Manhattan traffic was busy. Once he was in the back of the car, racing toward the hospital, his focus usually turned to the case ahead, the work he needed to do. But today, Emma overwhelmed his thoughts. Unexpected and unsettling. Part of him wished they'd woken up together, maybe stayed in bed a while and talked, enjoyed each other's company. But the other part of him knew that was both impractical and impossible. Impractical because he had to work. So did she. If he remembered correctly, she'd mentioned having a shift today in the ER. Impossible because regardless of the strange feelings he had toward her and the odd way he kept imagining what a future between them might look like, there was no way it could ever happen.

Sleeping together was nice. Way more than nice, actually. Amazing. But that's all it could ever be. What he'd told Emma about him not doing relationships still stood, even after their wonderful night together. And soon enough, Emma would realize what Thad had known all along. She deserved more than him. Deserved better than a grouchy recluse with serious boundary issues. She was sunshine and he was darkness. She saw the positive in everything, the good. She trusted people. He kept everyone at bay and trusted no one.

They were too different for it to ever work between them long-term.

Even if Emma had made him want to forget reality for a little while.

* * *

"I'll be waiting right here for you, Ms. Lovelace, when you get out. Promise," Emma said, holding the elderly woman's hand as they walked down the hall toward the OR. "And I'll check with social services, too, to see what we can do about help for you while you recover. Don't worry about a thing. Just get better."

"I'm here. Let's get the patient prepped," a familiar deep voice said, causing a shiver of awareness down Emma's spine. She looked up to see I had join the group of people flanking the gurney. His hair was a bit mussed, and his scrub top was on slightly crooked, but he still looked gorgeous to her. Their eyes caught from across the gurney and despite the situation, she couldn't help smiling at him.

Something flickered through his icy eyes— warm and comforting—before those too-familiar walls slammed back into place and his usual brusque demeanor returned. She should have been used to it by now, but after the intimacy they'd shared the previous night, her stomach still sank a little.

She returned to focus on the patient instead, who was gripping her hand like a lifeline. "Don't worry, Ms. Lovelace. There is no surgeon more capable in this city than Dr. Markson to handle your case. He's the best."

They hit the double doors into the OR then and Emma halted while the rest of them went through. Thad glanced up at her once more, their eyes locking briefly again before the doors closed and she was left alone in the now-silent hall.

Rather than wait for the elevator, she took the stairs, figuring the exercise would do her good and help keep her alert. To say she hadn't gotten much sleep last night would be an understatement, but she wouldn't have changed it at all. Dating and sex for her had been luxuries ever since she'd taken her sister in ten years ago. Between her busy schedule at work and handling a teenager, there wasn't much time for Emma to focus on herself and her needs. Usually, it didn't bother her. Flings and quickies here and there. No strings, no attachments. No real disruptions to the life she'd built for herself and Karley.

But then along came Thad. A man who many feared or loathed, but Emma found to be a squishy marshmallow beneath his arctic snowman exterior. Sure, he could be difficult and prickly and sometimes downright wrong, but couldn't everyone? She was an optimist, yes, but Emma wasn't naive. She knew trying to do any sort of normal "dating" with Thad would be hard with the weird obstacles they face—location, time, social circles—but still. The connection they had was strong, and rare, and Emma wasn't ready to consign it to the quickie pile just yet. They needed to talk about things once they had a moment in their busy days. Yep.

But that moment was a long time coming unfortunately. Because while Emma had been upstairs with Ms. Lovelace, apparently there'd been a gas leak in a building nearby and now the ER was running nonstop with all the new patients flooding in from that. Emma kicked into high gear, efficiently triaging patients into those who needed admits versus those who could be treated and released. The fact that they were chronically short-staffed didn't help either.

By the time they got the trauma rooms cleared and she had a chance to take a breather, it was afternoon. Emma clocked out and headed to the employee break room in the back of the ER to grab a bottled water. Then she checked with the OR to discover Ms. Lovelace was out of surgery and recovering well in the ICU, though still heavily sedated. She wouldn't wake up until the morning, so Emma didn't plan to go up and see her until then.

Back aching, she slumped into a chair in the otherwise empty break room and took a sip of her water. Her lack of sleep the night before was catching up with her now. She checked her smartwatch. Five more minutes of rest before she needed to go back. She closed her eyes just for a second, only to be awakened by that low, familiar voice again.

"You look tired," Thad said from the break room entrance, one shoulder leaned against the doorframe.

Emma opened on eye to peer at him. "So do you."

Which wasn't exactly true. Where she felt harried and probably looked a mess, Thad was back to his crisp, perfect, chilly self again. His hair combed and his pristine white lab coat in place over fresh blue scrubs. How a man could look that good after making love all night, then spending the morning in surgery, she had no clue. The only signs at all of his fatigue were the slight shadows beneath his eyes, but most people wouldn't notice because most people avoided making eye contact with him for fear he'd go Grinch on them. Not Emma, though. Not anymore.

"You should go home," he said, pushing

away from the doorframe to walk over to her table. "You can't get sick now. We've got too much to do for the carnival."

She yawned, then smiled. "I'm on until five. And I'm not going to get sick. Don't worry. I wouldn't leave you in a lurch. Sit down and share the last—" she checked her watch again "—two minutes of my break with me."

He sighed, then sank into the chair across from her. "Emma, about last night…"

Oh boy. Those words were never good. She straightened and clenched her water bottle tighter than necessary. "Thad, now really isn't a good time. Maybe we can meet up later, where we'd have more privacy?"

A small muscle ticked near his tense jaw as he gave a curt nod. "I just… I've been thinking a lot about us."

"Me, too." Honestly, she hadn't really stopped thinking about them. Maybe they could try to make this last if they were both willing.

His dark brows drew together. "I don't know what we're doing, Emma. None of this makes logical sense."

"I see." She shouldn't be disappointed, because it wasn't like he hadn't told her up front he didn't do relationships, but yet she was. This time had felt different for her. She thought it might be the same for Thad, too. Still, she tried to play down the growing sting of hurt inside her. "It doesn't have to make sense. We're two consenting adults who had a good time last night. That's all. I like you, Thad. I thought you liked me, too."

"I do like you, Emma." He looked at her then, his gaze panicked. "More than I should. More than I intended. And that's a problem for me because I don't do that sort of thing. I told you that." Thad licked his lips, his posture rigid. "I don't want you to get hurt, Emma. Do you understand?"

Emma watched him for a moment, frowning. "I'm a big girl, Thad. I can take care of myself. You won't—"

"But I will," he said, cutting her off, his tone taking on a desperate edge now. "I will hurt you, Emma. Eventually. Because I can't be what you need. I'm no good. I'm distant and aloof. I hate going to parties and being social. I prefer my quiet office and my dog to most people. That isn't the kind of life you want, is it? Isolated. Alone. People hurrying away when they see you coming. Because that's what it would be like with me, and you deserve better."

"Thad, come on." Emma tried to reach over

and take his hand, but he pulled away. She sat back and crossed her arms. "Look, I know you had a hard time with your father. I know you've got demons you're dealing with from the way he treated you. But we all have things we deal with. People can change if they want to. And I know that's not who you are inside. I've seen the real you, Thad, and you're wonderful."

"No, I'm not." He stood, his voice vehement now. "I'm not wonderful. You see what you want to see. You only see the good in others, Emma. But the truth is, the only good thing about me is my surgical abilities. Without those, I'm nothing. Therefore, my work always has and always will come first. It's the most important thing for me and there's no room for anything else. I'm not good for anything else."

Wow. Stunned, Emma just blinked at him. His father's lies had left scars even deeper than she'd realized. She cursed the dead man and how he'd made his son think so little of himself and what he had to give the world. Thad was amazing, both in and out of the operating room, but if he didn't believe it himself, there was no way she could convince him otherwise.

Her smartwatch beeped, meaning her break

was over. She took a deep breath and stood, pushing her chair in. "I have to go. We should talk about this more later. I'll text you when I'm done working and maybe we can meet up later."

"No." He crossed his arms, staring at the floor instead of her. "I don't think there's anything more to discuss about us. We should stick to the carnival plans from now on."

She closed her eyes and counted to ten before opening them again, surprised hurt scorching through her usually sunny outlook. Thad wasn't the only one who'd taken a chance last night. Up until now, Emma had steered clear of romantic entanglements, far too busy with work and focusing on her sister and getting promoted than love. And while she liked Thad—more than liked him, if she was honest—she was just as scared and uncertain of how quickly things had intensified between them. Sleeping with a man was one thing. Opening her heart and her past to him, as she had with Thad, was another. But if he couldn't see that or didn't value it, she refused to beg. "Fine. If that's what you want. Perhaps we should avoid face-to-face meetings then. Stick with texts and phone calls from here on out. We should be able to get the carnival finished that way."

"Yes. It is what I want, and I think your idea is a good one." He let out a slow breath, looked relieved. "I'm glad you understand."

"Actually, I don't." She shook her head. "But if you don't trust me enough to work through this, then there's no point."

"Em—"

"Stop," she interrupted, holding up her hand. "I need to work now. But let me end by saying I like you, Thad. A lot. And I thought last night was amazing. I'd like to explore that more with you. But you obviously don't so, fine, end of story."

He opened his mouth, as if to argue, then hung his head. "You can do better than me."

She nodded, projecting confidence even though she was crumbling inside. "You're right. I can."

She left the break room, and damn if those weren't some of the hardest steps she'd ever had to take. Because that connection between her and Thad still burned bright, urging her to go back and hug him, tell him that he was good, that there was hope, even though she knew there wasn't. He'd made his decision and there was no point arguing. Change happened fast and the best you could do was ride it out and try to keep your head above water. Emma knew that better than most. She'd lived it for the past ten years and survived. She should've known better than to veer out of the happy lane she was in.

Well, no more. If Thad was satisfied playing the Grinch of Fifth Avenue, then let him. She had more than enough to keep her busy. She had the carnival to plan for Ricky. She had Ms. Lovelace upstairs who needed her. She had Karley at home. She had a promotion to win here in the ER.

But what she didn't have was Thad Markson. And right then, he was the only thing that mattered.

CHAPTER NINE

"SIS, WHAT'S UP?" Karley asked, leaning her hip against the edge of the kitchen counter in their apartment. "You've been quiet for days and that's not like you. Didn't even try to cheer up cranky Mr. Lewis next door when he brought over the mail that got misdelivered."

Emma sighed and looked up at her younger sister, standing there with her arms crossed waiting for an answer. With the holiday rush, it had been a busy time for both sisters and today was the first day in a week they'd both been home together. Emma had hoped a quiet Sunday would help settle her before the last big push to get the carnival done. They had less than a week now until Christmas Eve.

"I'm fine," Emma said, trying not to let her inner sadness show. Seemed like an eternity ago now that she'd been with Thad, like a fairy-tale dream she'd wakened from too early. Or maybe too late. Either way, she was still reeling from their whiplash breakup and wasn't sure what to do about it. Part of her felt silly even calling it a breakup, considering they hadn't ever really been together—not in the relationship sense, anyway. But she missed him. Even with his prickly nature and lack of social skills and overall allergy to anything remotely bright and cheerful. Or maybe because of it.

Go figure.

The man couldn't be more different from her and yet they shared the same deep connection. A connection that still tugged at her heart each time her phone buzzed, hoping maybe it was Thad.

He'd stuck to their agreement, only contacting her by text or call, mainly the former. And damn if she hadn't caught herself glancing around the ER during her shifts this past week, trying to catch a glimpse of him. It was silly. It was infuriating. It was ridiculously confusing.

She was the happy one, the sunny person who made everyone else's day brighter. Like the Cindy Lou Who of Manhattan West. And she'd allowed her light to be snuffed, at least temporarily, by the Grinch of Fifth Avenue.

How in the world had that happened?

She didn't know.

All Emma did know for sure was she'd spent the last few nights since her fight with Thad tossing and turning, despite being bone-deep weary. Her usually pleasant dreams were haunted by memories of them together, his kisses, his taut, muscled body pressed against her, moving inside her, driving her to the heights of pleasure.

"Hello?" Karley stood beside the table now, waving a hand in front of Emma's face. "Earth to sis. Is this about your partner? The cute doctor who took you to that dance?" Karley crossed her arms, gaze narrowed on Emma, waiting for an answer. When one didn't come, her eyes widened. "Oh my God, sis! It is, isn't it?"

"What? No." Flushed and flustered, Emma shuffled the papers in front of her on the table, avoiding Karley's too-perceptive stare. "Of course not. We're just working on the carnival together. That's all."

"This conversation is inappropriate and I'm not having it with you." Emma did her best to refocus on her vendor lists, but it was no use. Her mind was too cluttered now with anxious adrenaline, and the words blurred before her eyes. "Don't you have homework or something to do?"

"Already done." Karley grinned and leaned forward, resting her forearms on the table, clearly not going anywhere. Perfect. Not. "So, you like this guy, huh? I can tell by the way you're acting."

"I'm not acting any way at all," Emma snapped, the heat in her face rivaling the surface of the sun. "And how I feel about Dr. Markson isn't important." *Not anymore.*

Her sister frowned now and sat back. "Why? Did he hurt you? Want me to go over there and smack him for you?"

"No!" Emma didn't look at Karley then. "He didn't hurt me. We just had a misunderstanding, that's all." Her chest squeezed tighter, and she swallowed hard before staring down at her papers again. Good Lord. She blinked hard against unexpected tears. She would not cry about this. Nope. Especially not in front of Karley. "I'm just under a lot of pressure right now to make sure this wish project turns out well, so I have a better shot at that promotion at work. After Christmas, I'll be back to normal. Promise."

Karley gave her a flat look. "You work harder than anyone I know, Em. You always put everyone else first, do whatever you can to make everyone feel better. But if this guy doesn't appreciate it, then he doesn't deserve you. End of story."

"Dr. Markson appreciates me," Emma said, rising to his defense though she didn't know why.

"Sure." Karley shook her head. "Whatever."

"He does. He's actually a really good man."

Her sister responded by raising a skeptical brow at her. "If he's so good, then why are you sitting here miserable now instead of being at his fancy Park Avenue town house with him?"

"Fifth Avenue," Emma corrected before she caught herself. "And you shouldn't judge someone just by where they live. Just because his family had money doesn't mean there aren't problems to go along with it."

"Maybe." Karley shrugged. "Is it nice there?"

"At the town house? Yes, very nice."

"Does he have servants?"

"A butler. Older man named Everett." It was Emma's turn to scowl now. "Why?"

"So it's just him and his butler living alone in that great big house?" her sister asked.

"Yes. Oh, and Thad has a service dog named Baxter."

"Service dog?" Karley perked up a little

at that. "Why would he need one of those? Is he sick?"

Oops. It wasn't her business to talk about Thad's illness. Realizing she'd said too much already, Emma stood and picked up her paperwork for the vendors. "I think I'm going to take a nap."

Her sister protested as Emma brushed past her. "Hey, sis. Don't get offended. I'm just trying to figure out why he's got you so torn and twisted."

"I'm not…" Emma's voice trailed off. She was tired. Exhausted, really. She sank onto the couch in their living room and buried her face in her hands, her voice sounding raw to her own ears as she said, "Please, just forget it. Okay?"

Karley joined her in the living room and put her arm around Emma's shoulders, pulling her into a much-needed hug. "Hey, it's okay, sis."

"No, it's not," Emma said, her words catching on a sob. God. This was not how it was supposed to work. Emma was the older one, the strong one, the one who should be comforting Karley, not the other way around. Yet she couldn't seem to stop her tears. "Everything's a mess."

Despite her wishes, the whole sad tale of

what had transpired between her and Thad over the past few weeks came tumbling out—well, except for the sleeping together part. Some things needed to stay private, even between sisters. Still, Karley was smart enough to connect the dots. Seventeen going on thirty indeed.

"Wow," her sister said, sitting back a short while later and pushing Emma's braids away from her face. "Yep. Sounds like a mess all right."

Emma laughed through her tears, swiping the back of her hand across her damp cheeks. "Thanks for agreeing with me." She sniffled, then shrugged. "It probably would've been easier to move on if we didn't still have to stay in contact because of the carnival, but little Ricky's depending on us and I won't let him down, so…"

"There's the Em I know." Karley smiled and got up, returning a minute later with a box of tissues from the bathroom. She handed them to Emma, then pulled one out to dab the tears from her sister's cheeks. "The optimist with a spine of steel. Honestly, I'm not an expert on men."

"That's good to know."

Karley gave her a look. "Seriously, though. It sounds to me like you need to take charge of the situation if you want to fix things with him. And you need to do it face-to-face. Go to his town house and talk to him."

"Oh, I don't know." She blew her nose, then scowled down at the tissue as she twisted it in her hands in her lap. "We agreed not to see each other again and he's so reclusive, I'm not sure how I'd even get in."

"Hmm." Karley sat back, her expression thoughtful as she stared at the coffee table. "What about those papers you're working on?"

"The vendors?" She blinked at the stack of papers she'd been working on earlier. "He hasn't given me the specifications for the site yet and it's getting down to the wire."

"That's good." Her sister nodded and grinned. "Go over and fib a little. Say you'd been trying to call him all day but couldn't get through. Tell him one of the vendors is pressing you for the specifications. Then when you get inside, sit him down and have a talk about things."

Before Emma could respond, Karley's phone buzzed.

"Need to take this. My bestie's having a man crisis, too." Karley leaned over and kissed Emma's cheek, then stood. "Good luck, sis. Can't wait to hear how it turns out."

Emma watched her sister walk away, then leaned back into the cushions and stared at the ceiling. She hated to break the agreement with Thad about sticking to phone communication only, but how else were they supposed to mend fences between them? And needing to know specifics about the venue was important. With only a week left until Christmas Eve, they did need to get confirmation from his foundation on the location for the carnival. So far, Thad had brushed her off when she'd asked, but as a partner on the project, she had a right to know. Still, she didn't feel right just showing up at his town house again, nor did she want to wait all day like he'd made her do before. She pulled out her phone and stared down at the screen, her stomach lurching. Should she text first? That would be easier. But no. He could ignore a text and it could come across wrong. Best to call and get it over with. She pulled up his number and waited as it rang once, twice…

"What?" Thad's deep, growly voice rolled down the line and over her like velvet and sin.

For a moment, Emma couldn't say a word. Then she blurted out, "It's Emma."

A pause. Thad exhaled slowly, sounding

about as worn out as she felt. "What do you need?"

You. I need you.

Emma gripped her phone tight, her heart slamming against her rib cage and her throat dry. "I need to speak with you about the vendors. We need specifications for the vendors so they will be able to set up properly," she said, praying she hid her nervousness well. "We only have a week left."

"I know how long we have left, Emma." His tone turned sharp. "Now is not a good time."

"Are you at the hospital?" she asked. Dammit. She really hadn't thought this through as well as she should have. If he was in the middle of an important case, she didn't want to interrupt him. "Sorry."

"What? No. I'm home. But I..." She heard the sounds of leather creaking and pictured him getting up from behind his desk in the study, pacing back and forth in front of the tree they'd decorated together. He cursed under his breath. "Fine. Yes. What time can you be here?"

"Half an hour?"

"Okay. I'll call my foundation and get as much information as I can from them. Have you eaten yet?"

The question took Emma by surprise. "Uh, no."

"Good. Everett serves dinner at six. Will that work?"

"Sure."

"See you then, Emma."

He clicked off and she sat there staring at the wall in her living room, stunned. It had worked. She and Thad were going to talk. About the carnival, but it was better than nothing. Pulse racing, she straightened and walked over to knock on Karley's bedroom door. Her sister was still on the phone but stopped as Emma stuck her head inside. "Can you do takeout for dinner?"

Karley nodded and gave her a thumbs-up. "Go get him, sis."

Around five forty-five Thad finished up the phone call with his foundation. They'd pulled a lot of strings to find a venue to meet their needs, but in the end, they'd managed to secure an amazing place. In fact, if everything came together as planned, they'd be able to invite not only the children from the PICU at Manhattan West, as Ricky wanted, but also all the other hospitals' PICUs in the city. Thad was nothing if not an overachiever and besides, it soothed an old wound inside him that had festered too long. Granting little Ricky's wish was like throwing the party Thad had always wanted as a child himself and never received.

Now that he'd solved one problem, he faced another. Emma.

Inviting her to dinner had probably been a mistake. He should have stuck to his guns and insisted they handle the carnival issues over the phone as they'd agreed. But man, the thought of seeing her again after time apart made his battered heart sing.

Which made no sense. For once since this whole debacle started with her, he'd thought rationally and acted from logic, not emotion, when he'd said they should work apart from now on. Then all it had taken was one phone call from her to crumble his resolve. How would he ever survive if he pushed her away again? How would he ever survive if he didn't?

Thad was still stewing over that dilemma when Everett knocked on his office door to announce, "Ms. Trudeau is downstairs, sir."

"Thank you," Thad said. "I'll be right down."

The butler left and Thad watched his old friend go, still concerned about the man's condition. Everett still had a slight limp and his coloring had not improved much. Thad had tried to get the older man to let him examine him again last night, but Everett had waved him off once more, stating he had an appointment with his own physician the next day and that it was nothing. In fact, Everett had insisted he felt better, even if he didn't look it.

Anxiety buzzed through his system even as he tried to tamp it down. Not just over Everett's condition but also the fact that Emma was there, in his home, once more. Not for a social call or date, but for business. He needed to remember that and keep his emotions out of it. Never mind that each time he closed his eyes, Thad remembered the feel of her beside him, beneath him, around him. Could still smell her spicy-sweet scent and taste her lips. He needed to forget those things. She wasn't meant for a man like him. Love wasn't meant for a man like him.

Resigned, he headed downstairs to find her already seated in the large formal dining room where Everett would serve dinner tonight. Normally, Thad ate in the kitchen where it was smaller and homier. But considering what had happened in there with Emma on the first night she'd been here, Thad didn't want reminders of the past to muddle things any more than they already were.

"Hello, Emma." Thad stopped on the threshold to meet her gaze down the length of the long mahogany table. She wore a silly red sweater tonight with Santa on the front and looked more beautiful than ever. Yearning constricted his throat and he swallowed hard against it, battling his rioting emotions. From the moment Emma Trudeau had entered his life, all of his ideas about himself and the world had exploded into a million pieces. She didn't think he was broken or a monster. She'd asked him for nothing except his help and his kindness. She had scars and had suffered hurt, but she used her pain to bring light to others, not hide away. She made him question his decisions, and for a man whose patients lived and died by those decisions, it was terrifying as hell.

"Thad?"

Her voice startled him back into motion. He headed for the chair across from hers. "Yes?"

"Are you okay?"

She watched him warily, like he might have another hypoglycemic episode. Dammit. He'd been in the same room with Emma for less than five minutes and already his plans for a quick professional meeting were derailing.

"I'm fine, thank you." He gave a curt nod to Everett, hoping to keep the rest of the evening on track. "We're ready for dinner."

The older man disappeared through a doorway into the kitchen, Baxter sticking to the butler's side like glue. Odd that, since he rarely left Thad's side when he was home, but Thad didn't have the brain space to worry about it now. They sat in awkward silence as Thad studied Emma from beneath his lashes. There were faint shadows under her eyes, suggesting she'd had sleepless nights, too. Before he could ask her, however, thankfully Everett returned with their meals, grilled salmon and quinoa, Baxter trotting beside him.

"So," she said, after thanking the butler, then placing her napkin atop her lap. "Did you speak with your foundation?"

"I did," he said, taking a sip of his water. "They've secured an excellent venue. One I hope you'll be as happy with as I am."

"Oh." She blinked at him, looking surprised. "Good. Where is it?"

"They actually originally had two that met our specifications. Large, good ventilation, heated." He ate a bit of salmon, watching her. "I settled on the second one. Madison Square Garden."

She froze with her fork halfway to her mouth, eyes wide. "The Madison Square Garden?"

"Yes."

"How… What…" Emma shook her head, setting her fork down carefully, then wiping her mouth before continuing. "Do we have the donations to cover that expense? I'm sure it's not cheap."

"Far from it." Thad smiled, satisfied that she seemed suitably impressed with his work. "And yes, we have the funds to cover the rental." *With my help.* "It took some finagling by my foundation, too, to get the Christmas Eve date we wanted for the arena. They wanted to use it for some sporting event, but I pulled some strings and now it's ours." He cleared his throat. "With the capacity, our vendors should have no problems setting up the booths and rides in there. And we could also invite more people."

"Who?"

"I'm thinking children and their families from other PICUs in the city."

"Uh, wow. Okay." She took another bite of her food and chewed slowly, as if considering all that he'd said. Then she looked behind her at Everett. "This food is excellent."

"Thank you, ma'am," the older man said, bowing a bit awkwardly.

Emma laughed, then shook her head. "You can call me Emma, Everett."

"As you wish, ma—" the butler stopped himself. "Emma."

Thad regarded their exchange with astonishment. In all the years Everett had been with him, he'd never asked the man to call him Thad. He felt bad about that now. Scowling, Thad shifted his attention back to Emma. "May I ask you a question?"

She ate a roasted carrot and Thad tried not to remember how soft her lips were. "Sure. If I can ask you one in return."

"Fine. How exactly do you remain so happy all the time?" He waved his fork around at the room in general. "Stay so friendly and open and joyful, with the state of the world?"

Emma didn't respond at first, her expression serious. "First of all, I'm not always happy, Thad. Some days are harder than others." He managed not to wince at the thinly veiled reference to their conversation in the break room the previous week. "But then I remind myself that I can't fix every problem in the world. All I can do is get up each day and improve my little corner of it. The rest is up to the universe."

"The universe?"

"Or God, or whatever you believe in that's bigger than you. Divine intelligence."

He shook his head, the idea of leaving anything up to chance only spiking his anxiety more. "I don't know what to do with your concept."

"I know." She gave him a small smile, her eyes kind. "But I always remember what my mother told me when I was little. Sometimes it's braver to surrender what you can't control."

Part of Thad recognized she was trying to get a point across to him. But another part, the part conditioned by his dead father to believe his worth came from the results he produced, balked.

Emma chuckled. "I think that's the first time I've seen you speechless."

He shook his head and finished the last bite of his food. "Your answer just surprised me, that's all."

"Hmm." She sat back for Everett to take her empty plate, then waited until the butler took Thad's as well and disappeared into the kitchen again before saying, "Now it's time for my question."

His heart skipped a beat and Thad gulped more water. "All right."

"I want to know the real reason you pushed me away."

Tell her. Tell her the truth. Let her see you for who you really are. Let her in. Open up.

It was the hardest thing he'd ever done, harder than losing his mother, harder than suffering his father's emotional abuse, harder than all those long nights in the hospital as a scared little boy alone. But he wanted this, needed this, needed her in his life, more than he needed his next breath.

"I—" he started, only to be cut off by a loud crash from the kitchen followed by the dog's frantic barks. Thad scowled, his attention snapping to the door behind Emma. "What the hell? Everett?"

No answer.

Anxiety soaring through the roof now, Thad was up out of his chair and pushing into the kitchen in a flash. "Everett, is everything—"

No. Everything was not all right. The details of the scene before him registered all at once, flooding his mind with information. Everett on the floor, unmoving and deathly pale. Baxter by his side, nudging the older man with his nose and crying plaintively. The heat of Emma as she ran into the kitchen behind him, then stopped short.

"Help me, Emma. Now!" Thad's medical training overrode his shock and he dropped to his knees on the tile, not caring about the shards from the broken dishes cutting into his knees.

"Call 911. We need an ambulance here now!" he yelled to Emma as he turned over his butler, noting the bluish tint to his lips and his greenish-gray complexion. He checked the older man's pulse and breathing and detected neither. Not good. Not good at all. "Then get down here and help me start CPR until they arrive."

His blood froze.

Please don't die on me. You're the closest thing I have to a father. Stay with me.

Thad ripped open the front of Everett's black butler jacket, then his shirt to reveal the man's bare chest. Then he placed his hands over Everett's sternum and began compressions, counting in his head. He thought back over the last week or so. The unusual limp in Everett's walk, his unhealthy pallor. Given the man's age and the fact that he was overweight, chances were high he had elevated blood pressure and heart disease. A stroke was highly possible. Thad cursed himself for not insisting on taking his butler to the doctor earlier.

"EMS is on the way," Emma said, kneeling on Everett's other side and tipping the man's head back to clear his airways, and began giving him lifesaving breaths. "Had he been feeling unwell lately?"

"Yes. This is my fault," he growled, checking for a pulse again and this time finding one—thready and weak. "He's been limping for the past few days. And he didn't look good. But I let him brush me aside instead of taking him to the doctor. If he dies…"

No. That last thought was too horrible to bear. He couldn't let Everett die. Wouldn't let him die.

Sirens grew louder outside and Emma rushed to the door to let the EMTs in, a hand on Baxter's collar to keep him out of the fray. As the paramedics worked to get Everett stabilized and onto a gurney, Thad gave them his assessment. If it was a stroke, which he suspected it was, time was of the essence. "Take him to Manhattan West. I'll call one of my colleagues and have them meet us there."

Emma accompanied them to the door. "I'll follow you."

"No."

Dammit. He hadn't meant to say that as harshly as he had. But he was stressed and sick with worry and berating himself for being so self-absorbed that he'd allowed this situation to get to the point it had. Thad turned to see Emma's stricken expression. "I have to go." He glanced out the door to the ambulance at the curb where the EMTs were loading Everett into the back. "I'll check in with you later and give you an update."

Then he was running down the sidewalk, barely stopping to tug on his coat before climbing into the back of the rig and hurtling toward the hospital, the life of the man who'd taught him what it meant to be a real man, one who loved and cared for others more than themselves and their own comfort in life, in dire jeopardy.

CHAPTER TEN

EMMA GLANCED OUT the window of Thad's office upstairs, watching the lightly falling snow glittering the air over Central Park in the distance, her phone in hand. Karley was on the other end of the line, sounding about as stunned as Emma felt.

"He what?" her sister asked.

"Rented out Madison Square Garden arena for our carnival." Even saying it sounded unbelievable. Or maybe that was just her shock from seeing poor Everett lifeless on the kitchen floor. She was a medical professional, yes, but when disaster struck close to home, no one was immune.

"Isn't that wildly expensive?"

"Probably." Emma shook her head, still trying to wrap her brain around what had happened that night. "But the reason I called was to let you know I won't be home tonight.

I'm heading to the hospital to be there for Thad and Everett."

"So you guys made up then?"

"No. Not exactly." She rubbed her throbbing temple. "But Everett is all Thad has in this world and if he doesn't make it, Thad will need all the support he can get. Even if it's from me."

"Emma," Karley said. "I appreciate you want to help, but if he doesn't want you there…"

"I've got a shift in the morning anyway," she said, swiveling back to stare at the tree across the room, still glowing cheerfully as if Thad's world hadn't avalanched down around him tonight. "So once I check on him, I'll just start early. I'm sure they can use the help in the ER. You be okay by yourself?"

"I'm fine," her sister said. "Just don't do too much, okay? I know you want to help, but don't force it. Give him time to accept it."

"I will." Emma could picture her sister's dubious stare in her head. "I promise. Make sure the doors are locked before you go to bed."

"I'm not seven anymore, sis. I got this."

"I know." She started to end the call, then added. "I love you."

"Love you, too," Karley said. "And call me

with an update when you know something. I don't know the old man, but still. That's no way for a person to go."

"Will do."

Emma ended the call, then sank down into Thad's chair behind the desk. Baxter walked over and nudged her hand with his wet nose for a pet. Poor thing was probably still as traumatized as the rest of them. She smiled down at the dog, scratching behind his ears. "I know. You were such a good boy, Baxter. Alerting us to trouble."

The dog snuffled and whined, then lay down with his head on Emma's foot.

She sat there for a while, thinking of all the things they could do with the new venue. Thad had mentioned inviting all the kids and parents from the other PICUs in New York, and that was a great idea. They'd have to make provisions, based on each child's illness, and perhaps group them accordingly. Maybe stagger the times of entry to the carnival to accommodate everyone without crowding people too close together. There was still a lot of work to do, but Emma could handle it. Thad had done more than enough getting the venue.

And wow, what a venue it was.

Determined not to let his hard work and

sacrifice go to waste, and knowing he'd have more than enough to deal with over the next few days regardless of Everett's outcome, she sat forward and started jotting down lists of things to do on a pad of paper sitting atop Thad's desk. Okay. With the new area to cover, they would need more spotlights set up so people could see properly. They'd planned to hold the carnival for four hours, but if they were inviting more people and staggering the entries, they'd need more time. She would need to ask Thad for a contact person at the arena the next time she talked with him, so she could get schematics for the event. Hard to believe in less than a week, they'd transform Madison Square Garden arena into a winter wonderland and make little Ricky's dreams come true.

Hard to believe I've fallen for the Grinch...
The thought caught Emma off guard, but not because of her feelings for Thad. Tonight, when her heart had broken for him at his anguished pleas for Everett to stay with him as they performed CPR on the man together, Emma knew her caring for Thad went deeper than platonic. How deep exactly? She wasn't sure yet. But the emotions were there for her—warm and wonder-filled and full of future possibilities just the same. Time

would tell if those emotions went anywhere or if Thad felt the same toward her.

The one thing Emma was certain of, though, having worked with Thad these past few weeks, was that he wasn't the man everyone thought he was. He wasn't a Grinch. People at the hospital seemed genuinely surprised to learn from Emma how helpful he'd been on the project, and she secretly hoped this could lead to a new beginning for Thad at Manhattan West, if he wanted it. A fresh start, free from the burdens and fears heaped on him by his horrible, abusive father. Thad deserved to be welcomed and praised for what he was now—a successful, highly skilled surgeon and a generous philanthropist—not for the antisocial ways he'd shielded himself from his painful past.

And Emma intended to help with that transformation of his image, whether Thad wanted to continue seeing her after the project was over or not. In the same way he'd used his personal resources to secure the perfect venue for their carnival. Not because of any hope of reward, but because it was the right thing to do.

If that didn't prove he wasn't truly a Grinch, Emma didn't know what did.

She returned to the kitchen to make sure

Baxter had enough food and water to last him until someone could return to the town house the next morning, then took him out back into the gardens to potty before grabbing her coat from the closet off the foyer Everett had hung it in. Everett. She prayed once more the man would be all right and make a full recovery. He was the closest person in Thad's life. The only person in Thad's life that Emma knew of. Well, besides her now. And she wasn't going anywhere. Not without a fight.

Emma locked up the town house, then used the fresh air and exercise to hone her focus. She was about a block away from his place when her phone rang. Thad's number flashed on her caller ID. Heart in her throat, she answered. "What's happening?"

"They're still running tests, but they think it was a stroke," Thad said, a bit breathless. She imagined him pacing the halls of the hospital, his hair a mess from running his fingers through it and his cheeks flushed from adrenaline and stress. She wished she could be there now to hug him and show support. To tell him everything would be okay, even if it wouldn't. "My colleague Dr. Kinkaid is handling the case. He's the best in the business, besides me, so I trust him."

I trust him.

The words were bittersweet for Emma. She was glad Thad had found a good doctor to treat Everett, but she hoped someday Thad might trust her, too. It felt like the holy grail with him, being vulnerable and trusting. They weren't there yet, but maybe someday.

"I'm glad Everett's in capable hands." She meant it. The old butler had always been kind to her, and he'd helped tremendously during Thad's initial hypoglycemic attack. And despite their rather formal arrangement, the fact that Everett had stayed by Thad's side all these years had shown a loyalty and caring you had to admire. She couldn't imagine what Thad must be going through right now. "How are you doing?"

"I'm fine," he said, far too quickly.

"Thad. I don't believe that." Emma kept her tone low and calm, but firm. "Stop trying to be strong here. I was there when we did CPR on him, I could see the fear on your face. Everett is your friend, your confidant, your closest companion. You said as much yourself. This had to be traumatic for you."

The squeak of his shoes on the floor that had echoed through the phone line since the start of their conversation stopped, letting her know he stood still now. "It's my fault. I saw signs he hadn't been up to par the past few days and I let him dismiss them with me. I'm a doctor and his employer. I should have insisted he go in for treatment."

"What? No. None of this is your fault." Emma had seen it more than enough times in the ER. People blaming themselves because of "if onlys." If only they'd done this or that. If only they'd responded soon or made a different decision. Hindsight was always twenty-twenty. But she feared Thad would try to suppress all of his rediscovered emotions over this and retreat back into the safety of his cold, lonely, emotionless cave again. "Everett was a grown man, and while he worked for you, you were not the boss of him personally, no matter what you might think. He needs you now, Thad. Be here for him, the way he's been there for you from the start."

Thad didn't respond at first and Emma feared she'd gone too far. Then he sighed. "I need to get back to his exam room. They'll be taking him up to surgery soon."

"I'm on my way into the ER now," she said. "Figured I'd start my shift early since I'm already up. I'll try to find you later and see how things are going. If you need me for any reason before then, you know where to find me."

"Thanks, Emma," he said, his voice rough and strained. "For everything."

The call ended then, leaving Emma at the top of the steps leading down into the subway terminal, blinking tears away hard. It was still hours until dawn, but she prayed for light anyway.

Everett's surgery turned out to be long and hard, including an emergency craniotomy to relieve pressure on his brain from the subarachnoid hemorrhage and the neurosurgeon clipping the vessels that had ruptured. The next several hours in recovery would be crucial to determine how successful the procedure had been and whether Everett would ever regain consciousness.

Thad had spent the two hours his old friend was in the OR wearing a hole in the carpet of the waiting area, stewing over everything that had happened the past few weeks with Emma, and with Everett for his entire life. All the tumultuous feelings of guilt and shame and hope and yearning left him weary to his bones. But Emma had been right. Everett had been there for him all these years. He couldn't leave the older man now. Wouldn't leave him.

Please, Everett. Stay with me.

He sat in the private ICU room he'd secured for Everett, by the man's bedside. Monitors beeped around him and from somewhere down the hall, through the open doorway, he heard far-off hushed conversation at the nurses' station. Thad closed his eyes for a moment and pictured Emma, downstairs in the ER, helping patients feel better. Knowing she was there, at Manhattan West, made him feel better, too. Outside the windows across from him, the first rays of sunlight pierced the horizon with streaks of pink and gold and purple. A new day had arrived.

Time ticked by and Thad's eyes grew heavy. He didn't sleep, but he did reminisce. About all the times Everett had helped him when he'd been younger. Teaching him how to take care of his blood sugar. Tutoring him on his homework. Comforting him after the endless fights with his father.

Those memories soon morphed into his more recent times with Emma. The first night he'd seen her in his kitchen, mistaking her for an angel. The fundraiser, breathtaking in her red gown. Decorating the tree in his office. Visiting young Ricky in the

PICU. Their first kiss behind the Christmas tree in the lobby. The second kiss in his office. Making plans for the project. Making love in his bed.

Emma had seared herself in his life, into his heart, without him realizing it and now he wasn't sure how he'd ever let her go. They only had a few days left until the carnival and then she'd be gone, and his life would return to the same sad, dreary, lonely existence it had been before.

His eyes opened and he sat up straighter. Did he want that? No. He didn't. But how to change that? Circumstances were still the same as they had been. Thad had opened up a lot more during his time with Emma, but he was still a busy surgeon with a demanding schedule and a penchant for solitude. He couldn't ask Emma to change for him. She loved people. Loved being out in the world experiencing new things and new ideas. He preferred the safety of his office and ordered searches on his computer. And there was her sister to consider, too. She still had a family, a life, separate from his. How would that work? Would they, could they, blend the two? If Everett survived, he'd need help and care at the town house to recover. Thad was happy to provide that for him or hire someone to do that, but it would require even more of his precious free time, leaving even less to spend with Emma after this project.

Most of all, though, he feared she'd had enough of him. Enough of his isolation and grumpiness. Enough of his wariness and pushing new things away. Deep down, he knew that it wasn't her who needed to change here. It was him. But was he capable of it? Even for Emma?

Everyone loses something in life eventually... It's how we choose to deal with it that matters... I choose to be happy.

Her words looped in his head, urging him to try. Was it that simple, though?

Thad wasn't sure. The only thing he was sure of at the moment was that Emma was everything he never knew he needed. Fate had brought them together through some Christmas miracle and now that he'd found her, he never wanted to let her go. Could he change himself enough to keep her, though? To make her happy, as she'd made him? To allow her to see him, really see him, with no filters, no barriers, no fear, and to do the same for her?

It would be the most difficult thing he'd ever done in his life, including his delicate surgeries, but he wanted to try. For Emma. For himself. For the future they might have together.

If she'd still have him.

"Thad?" Her quiet voice carried from the doorway as if conjured by his thoughts.

He straightened in his seat and gave her a tentative smile, gesturing to the chair beside his, his pulse pounding in his head. "Come in, Emma."

"How is he doing?" she asked, looking at Everett in the hospital bed, tubes and wires attached to him, the rhythmic whoosh and hiss of the ventilator keeping him breathing and alive. "The surgery went well, I hope."

"As well as can be expected," Thad said, grateful for her warmth beside him as Emma settled into her chair. She was wearing scrubs again and her braids were tied back at the nape of her neck. She looked tired and over-worked and so beautiful it made his chest ache. He forced his attention back to Everett. "We got him here quickly after the stroke, which is crucial, and they began anticoagulation therapy fast. That, plus the surgery should minimize the damage from the bleeding on his brain, hopefully. We won't know the extent of his injuries, though, until he wakes up."

If he wakes up...

Thad swallowed hard and stared at the monitors for fear he'd break down completely. This was like losing his mother all over again. Except this time, he knew what was happening and there was no Everett to comfort him because his old friend was the one who was sick.

Then Emma took his hand, entwining his cold fingers with her warm ones and squeezing gently. "I'm sure this is very scary and painful for you, Thad. But please know I'm here for you. Whatever you need. Just let me know."

Normally, he took such things as flippancy. Stuff people said to make themselves feel better when they didn't know what else to do. It had happened after his mother had died, and even now, his colleague had mentioned the same today when he'd filled Thad in after the surgery. Thad knew better than to take them at their word. But now...

Let her see you... No filters, no barriers, no fear...

His earlier realization came to bite him in the butt. He wanted to let her in, wanted to rely on her, wanted to accept her support, her caring. The fear part, though, was strong.

Do it anyway.

Those words were in Everett's voice in his head. Nudging him toward the truth.

And the truth was, these two people had become his family. Small and odd, maybe, but still. Everett and Emma were the two people he'd let closest to him in the world. And family wasn't by blood, necessarily, it was who you trusted. Who was there for you no matter how difficult the situation, or how terribly you screwed up. People who had your back and you had theirs.

People like Everett and Emma.

"I want you to be here," he blurted out before he could stop himself. "I... I want your help and your friendship and whatever else you want to give me, Emma. And I want to give that back to you, too, tenfold, a thousandfold. Anytime, anywhere. Anything I can do, just name it. I just... I don't want this to be over."

Emma just looked at him for a long moment, and he cringed inside. Man, he was so bad at this stuff. Probably because he had no framework to base it on. And the man who'd always advised him on matters of emotion and the heart couldn't currently tell him how to handle this.

Finally, though, she laughed. It was the last thing Thad had expected and the thing he'd needed most right then. The awful tension and gloom in the air shattered like icicles, raining down prismatic rainbows of hope through the quiet ICU room. Even Everett's color and vitals improved and for the first time in forever, Thad felt a rush of something very akin to optimism.

It filled him to bursting, like his heart had grown three sizes bigger in a matter of seconds, filling him with happiness and joy and peace regardless of the circumstances. Not unpleasant, per se. But definitely different from his usual reserve.

"Oh, Thad." Emma cupped his cheeks, then leaned in to kiss him right there in the ICU and he didn't even care. "I'll stay as long as you want me. Promise."

He kissed her again then, just because he wanted to and it felt so good, then they sat side by side in Everett's room, holding hands and leaning their heads together.

"Does he have anyone we should notify?" Emma asked after a short while. "I can call them after I get back downstairs from my break."

"No. Not that I know of," Thad whispered. "He told me once he was married, back when I was still a baby, long before my mother died."

"What happened to his wife?" she asked, her tone sounding a bit sad.

"Cancer. She died at thirty," he said. "Way too young." Thad nestled closer to her warmth, more grateful than he could say to have her there beside him. More hopeful than he'd ever been that his future might be different from the vast empty desert he'd pictured for himself. "I don't think he ever tried to find anyone else after that." Thad shrugged, remembering what Everett had told him during that conversation. "He said when it's right, it's right."

Emma raised her head then to look at Thad, leaning in to kiss him softly. "Everett's a wise man."

"Yes," Thad agreed. "He really is."

Eventually, Emma had to leave the peace of the ICU and return downstairs to the controlled chaos of the ER. Good thing, too, because the first patient she walked into an exam room to see was her friend. "Ms. Lovelace? What are you doing back here?"

"My Christmas tree topper was crooked," the older woman said, shaking her head. "That nice young man from the community center came and put it up for me last week after I got home from my surgery. The star wasn't right. And since I live by myself, I had to fix it."

"Oh, dear." Emma gave the elderly woman a look. "Why didn't you call me? Or Karley? We're just down the block."

"Because you're busy, dear." Ms. Lovelace looked at her like it was obvious. "And New York blocks are long. Anyway, I got out my stepladder and climbed up. Almost had it, too, except the tree tipped."

"And you fell." Emma sighed, looking over the chart on her tablet. "You could've injured yourself badly."

"I'm fine." The older woman waved her off. "Only reason I'm here is the fellow who drops off my meals found me and panicked. Apparently, I passed out for a bit."

A bit? Emma read through the story the community center worker had given the EMTs who'd brought Ms. Lovelace in. According to the notes, the older woman had been unconscious for an undetermined amount of time. Not good. Rather than argue with her, though, Emma just nodded, then headed for the door. "All right. Let me find a doctor to examine you. I'll be right back."

By the time she'd corralled a busy resident, then called down both a neurologist and an orthopedic surgeon for consults and ordered all the tests and images both doctors wanted, more than a couple hours had passed. According to the clock on the wall, it was closer to noon now than morning, and Emma was ready for another break to see Thad again and check on Everett. What had happened upstairs earlier had been...amazing. Astounding. Absolutely better than she'd ever imagined things going.

But she was still concerned about pushing him too far, too soon. With the situation with Everett still in the balance, Thad was running on fumes both emotionally and energywise. And sometimes decisions you made and things you said when under duress, you regretted later. She never wanted him to regret anything they'd done or said together, so she'd be patient and wait. Emma was good at waiting.

She finished typing up her notes on Ms. Lovelace's case, then clocked out and headed for the elevators. But when the doors opened, Thad nearly ran her down in his haste to exit.

"Hey," she said, grabbing him by the arm, her stomach plummeting at his harried expression. "What's going on? Is it Everett?"

"Yes," he said, his words falling out in a tumble. "He's awake."

"Oh, Thad!" She threw her arms around

him and hugged him tight. Not caring that they were in eyesight of the ER and her nosy coworkers might see. She didn't care what they thought. All she cared about was Thad at that moment. "That's wonderful."

"Yes, it is," he said, holding her tighter for a moment before pulling back. "The neurosurgeon is examining him now, so I thought I'd come tell you."

"I was just on my way up," she said, moving slightly to the side as the other elevator dinged and a couple of techs wheeled off a patient. "Oh, Ms. Lovelace," Emma said. "You remember Dr. Markson?"

"Of course," the older woman said to him. "Back again, just in time for the holidays."

"What happened?" Thad asked, glancing between Emma and the patient. "Not your heart again."

"Nope. Fell off a stepladder," Ms. Lovelace said. At Thad's raised brow she added, "I'm fine. Sore and a bit stiff today. My head hurts, too, but I think I'm okay."

"How about we let the doctors be the judge of that, eh?" Emma shook her head, then chuckled.

"I'm in my eighties, child," the patient scolded Emma, though there was no sting in it. "I know my own body."

"Hmm." Thad looked her over quickly, then asked, "What day is it?"

"December nineteenth. I know that because I've got gifts being delivered five days from now on Christmas Eve. Had to pay an arm and a leg for them to get there that fast, too, but what are you going to do?"

Thad glanced over at Emma, biting back a smile. Seemed he really was a different man than before. The old Thad would never have smiled in front of a patient. "Very good on the date. You should really be more careful, though, Ms. Lovelace. You're still healing from the surgery I did for you, and at your age one fall could spell disaster. No more ladders."

"I know, I know." She waved him off, too. "But I'm old, Doc. Not dead. I can still do things."

"I'm sure you can. You're tough, Ms. Lovelace. I know that firsthand, but you're not invincible." He winked down at the older woman. "Next time perhaps wait until this Daniel from the community center comes by again, then ask him to help you."

Ms. Lovelace harrumphed. "He only comes three days per week, and I don't have the patience."

"Patience is hard, it's true." Thad leaned a

hip on the edge of the patient's bed, catching Emma's gaze once more. "But sometimes, the things we wait longest for are the best ones."

Yes, they are.

Emma cheeks heated and she looked away fast, but not before Ms. Lovelace's shrewd gaze caught her. The older woman glanced between her and Thad, a knowing look in her eyes. "Ah. Right. Yep. Waiting definitely has its benefits. I see your point, Doc, and I promise I'll think about it."

The techs rolled the patient back toward the ER and she and Thad stepped into a private consult room nearby for a moment. Once inside with the door closed behind them, Thad pulled her into his arms again to kiss her, then hold her close. They just stood there, holding each other for a long while. Finally, he pulled away and they sat down at the tiny table for two in there, Emma's heart still spinning from all the new possibilities between her and Thad.

He pulled his chair around in front of her, then sat down, putting them face-to-face. "You look tired."

"Gee, thanks."

"I'm exhausted, too. But you're still beautiful, Emma." His icy blue eyes were now lit with earnest fire. "The most beautiful woman I've ever seen."

Still, she tried to play it off, not used to such blatant compliments. "Stop flattering me."

"Not flattery. Truth." He took her hands in his. "I should probably wait to talk about all this with you, but it feels too important."

"What does?"

"What I'm feeling. What I realized sitting upstairs watching over the man I love like a father and praying he'd survive."

The sincerity in his tone sent ripples of tenderness through her. "You said Everett had woken up. That's a good thing, right? I mean, recovery might take a while but—"

"No, no. I know." He frowned. "I'm very relieved about that, believe me. But there's more. I realized sitting next to his bedside that he's my family, Emma, not my employee. That even though Everett and I are not related by blood, the bond we share is stronger than that. He's been there for me when no one else was."

"Oh." Emma blinked, taking that in, a sharp, unwanted pinch in the center of her chest. She was happy for Thad. She was. Happy that he'd realized that he did have a support system, people who cared for him and would support him, no matter what. That was so important. She had that with Karley, too. But there was still that part of her wishing she and Thad shared those feelings about each other. That it wasn't one-sided on her part. When he'd brought her in here and hugged her, she'd thought maybe he'd confess to wanting that same connection with her, too. Beyond the great sex and the great partnership they had on the project. Still, she didn't want to let her disappointment show. This was a big day for Thad, and he deserved the joy at his discovery. "That's wonderful."

He tilted his head and narrowed his gaze. "But?"

"But nothing," she added with faux cheerfulness. "I'm so glad you found family with Everett. You'll both need to rely on that for the next couple of months as he recovers."

"True." He stroked his thumbs over the inside of her wrists and Emma stifled a shiver. "I was hoping you might help, too."

Right. She was a nurse. She should've expected this. "I'm happy to assist in whatever he needs, Thad. But I might also be busier, too, if I get the promotion I want." Honestly, she hadn't really thought about the new job at all the past few weeks. She'd been so wrapped up with the carnival and with Thad, she'd lost sight of her original goals for taking on the project in the first place. At first, she hadn't cared so much, thinking she was building something more important than a promotion with him. But now, perhaps her decision to put him before her goals had been a mistake. Especially if he was only including her in his future as nursemaid to Everett.

Hollow and hurt, she checked her watch, then stood. "I, uh, I should probably get back to work."

"Emma," Thad said, holding on tight to her hands and shaking his head fiercely. "Please, don't go. I know I'm not handling this right at all. Saying all the wrong things at the wrong time instead of what I really feel. But all of this is new to me. No excuse, but it's the truth."

Suffering emotional whiplash and her lack of sleep and stress catching up with her, Emma's patience snapped its tether. She slumped back down in her chair, exasperated. "Oh, Thad. Just say it already. You know me. I won't judge you or berate you or whatever else you fear might happen. After all we've been through here, can't you trust me now?"

"I'm trying," he said, scowling down at their joined hands. "But I'm so used to protecting myself, to not being vulnerable. Trust is hard. But I realize I've been living on autopilot. Not really living at all. And life is so short. What happened with Everett drove that home for me. I've been so wrapped up in my past and my pain and my career that I missed so much." He looked up at her then and cupped her cheek. "So wrapped up that I almost missed the best thing that ever happened to me."

Emma struggled to understand what he was saying, her pulse racing harder than Santa's reindeer. "I care about you, too, Thad. I hope I've shown that over the past few weeks. I told you I wanted to continue seeing you after the project was over, but you shut me down." Despite her wishes, tears ran down her cheeks and she wiped them away with his thumb. "I can't do this alone, Thad. Relationships needs trust. And they need two people who are committed to making them work. I'm there, but only if you're fully there with me. Otherwise, I can't." She sat back, needing to get this out before she couldn't. "You think you're the only one who's scared here? I've lost people in my life, too, Thad. You know that. And while I've coped differently with it than you have, I really don't want to lose anyone else I care about, including you. But I will, if you're not ready to do this thing with me. Because it's going to take both of us putting one hundred percent into making it work. All day, every day. Rain or shine. Are you willing to do that, Thad? If not, please respect me enough to tell me."

He took a deep breath, hesitating, then nodded. "Yes, Emma. I'm ready. I'm terrified, but I'm willing to do whatever it takes to make this work because if feels too precious not to." He leaned his forehead against hers. "I have that same wobbly, shaking feeling I did that first night in my kitchen." At her worried look, he laughed. "I'm not hypoglycemic now though, I promise. One of the nurses upstairs brought me a meal and made sure I ate it all. My blood sugar is fine." He inhaled deep through his nose and his gaze turned serious. "This time it's all because of you, Emma. In the short time I've known you, you've taken everything I thought I knew, everything I thought I was, and turned it on its head. With you, all bets are off. My filters are gone. I feel things, say and do things before my logical brain can react. I lose control around you, and I like it." He kissed her gently. "I want to keep feeling this with you for as long as you'll have me. It's far too soon to tell where this will end up, but for now, I want you to know, Emma

Trudeau, that I care about you very much, and I'd like to date you."

She bit her lip, then burst into happy tears. "You silly, silly man. I care about you, too. And yes. I will date you."

"Good. That's settled then." Thad kissed and hugged her, and her tension dissipated under the flood of relief in her body. He'd taken a chance with her, and she couldn't have asked for more. In fact, she didn't want to ask for more. Not yet, anyway. Because sometimes the very best things came from the most unexpected places.

CHAPTER ELEVEN

ON CHRISTMAS EVE, just after sunset, Emma and Thad walked into the arena of Madison Square Garden and entered a dazzling, enchanted winter wonderland. The carnival vendors and ride owners had worked with the arena staff to pull off an incredible feat of both engineering and magic. From the Ferris wheel and the carousel they'd set up inside the space, to the snow falling gently around them from the artificial snow makers perched in the rafters, it was amazing. Most spectacular was the fact that it was all accessible to every one of the children, regardless of their situation.

"We did it," Emma whispered to Thad as they stood near the edge of the festivities, watching as the families of the PICU patients from around the city made their way around the carnival.

"Yes, we did." He kissed her sweetly, his

hand atop hers on his forearm. Thad still couldn't quite believe that he'd finally, after all these years, done something to prove he was worth something outside of his surgical skills. They'd made little Ricky's wish come true, because of all the hard work and effort of the woman beside him. The same woman he now got to call his girlfriend. There'd been so many lonely nights where he'd stood at the window in his office, watching life pass him by, fearing he'd never be a part of it. Not knowing how to be a part of it. But Emma had shown him the way. She'd given him a path to return to life. And that was a gift he could never repay.

"Look over there," she said, pointing at two giant snowmen near the carousel, greeting the riders as they waited for their turn. "Did you hire them?"

"I did." He grinned. "Well, actually my foundation did, since I've been busy with surgeries all week. But I gave them carte blanche to get the very best the city had to offer."

"Nice." They began walking the circuit around the carnival, nodding to families as they passed. Near the center of the enormous arena floor, a small ice rink had been set up as well for the kids to enjoy. Enough snow had fallen now, too, that people were making snowballs and snow angels. Thad had worried it would be a mess to clean up afterward, but the staff had assured him it was not a problem.

As they neared the carousel area, tinkling Christmas tunes drifted their way and they stopped in front of it to watch and listen. It was a beautiful piece of early twentieth-century art, with the carved wooden horses painted in bright, vivid colors, with polished gilded poles. Interspersed with the ponies were winter carriages and sleds large enough for wheelchairs.

"It's so beautiful," Emma gasped, clapping her hands. "We should ride it later."

Thad wrapped his arms around her waist and pulled her back into him, resting his chin atop her head. "We should. Do you think the carnival turned out well?"

She turned to gaze at him. "I think it turned out perfect. Thank you for helping me."

His pulse skyrocketed at the words, and he swallowed hard. "No, Emma. Thank you. This was all you from start to finish. I just got the venue."

Even with all his epiphanies and moves forward in his private life, coming here tonight had been a bit of a struggle, he wasn't going to lie. Socializing with so many people was a lot for him, but he refused to let Ricky and his parents down and he'd summoned his courage. Because with Emma by his side, he could do anything.

Eventually, they continued on around the arena floor, stopping at vendor booths to buy hot chocolates or check out the items they had for sale. Emma even won a stuffed dog at one of the games. Thad did his best to soak up all the sights and sounds of childhood heaven he'd been denied as a kid. The scents of cotton candy, hot dogs, popcorn and fried doughnuts. The colorful game booths showing off huge silly toys for prizes. Music blasting through the speakers, and his eyes dazzling with the blinking array of rides and ornaments and tinsel for the season. Delight and satisfaction swelled inside him.

We did this. Together.

His only regret was that Everett wasn't here to enjoy it with them. But he was doing better, awake and alert and even speaking again, though with a slight slur. The doctors expected him to make a full recovery in time, with help and lots of rehab. Thad intended to be by the man's side for all of it.

"Oh, look who's over there." Emma pointed. "Dr. Franklin and Jane Ayashi from HR. And they're with Ricky Lynch and his family. We should go say hello."

She tugged on his hand but for a moment Thad couldn't move, couldn't breathe, as a long-forgotten memory rushed back. His mother had brought him to a carnival like this as a small boy, before everything had gone sideways in his life. They'd had such fun, just him and his mother, and if he listened closely, he swore he heard the lilt of his mother's laughter on the air, like a sign he was on the right path now. For himself and for the future. Thad closed his eyes and said a silent thanks to his mother, or fate, or whoever had brought Emma into his life. She'd given him back his heart. His soul. She meant everything to him.

"Well, well," Dr. Franklin said as they approached. "You both pulled it off. Congratulations."

"Thank you," Emma said, squeezing Thad's hand. "We make a pretty good team. Just like I thought."

"Hmm." Dr. Franklin nodded at Thad. "I never knew you had it in you, Dr. Markson."

"That makes two of us," Thad joked, and they all laughed.

"It really is amazing." Jane Ayashi beamed, looking around at it all. "Can't imagine what it took for the two of you to pull this off so quickly."

"Elbow grease," Emma said, winking at Thad. "And a whole lot of trust."

"Exactly." Thad kissed Emma's mittened knuckles, ignoring the looks of their two colleagues.

"Dr. Markson, how is your friend in the ICU?" Dr. Franklin asked. "I heard it was thanks to your and Nurse Trudeau's quick reactions that he's still alive."

"Yes." Thad straightened, taking a deep breath. "Everett's awake and alert and from the last report I got earlier from his neurosurgeon, he should make a full recovery. I plan to move him out of Manhattan West as soon as he's ready and set up a private rehab unit in my town house for him."

Before anyone could ask more questions, a small, excited voice broke into their conversation.

"Dr. Markson!" Ricky Lynch yelled, running up with his parents. For someone so sick, Thad was astounded at the kid's energy. Then again, it was a magical night, and this carnival was proof miracles could happen, if you just believed enough. Ricky hugged

Thad first, then Emma, his pale cheeks flushed with excitement. "Thank you, thank you for my wish. It's more than I ever imagined."

"You're welcome, Ricky." Thad patted the boy's back, then straightened to shake his parents' hands. "And it's good to finally meet you, Mr. and Mrs. Lynch."

"Same," Ricky's dad said, shaking Thad's hand, then putting his arm back around his wife's shoulders. "Our son was just enrolled in a new clinical trial for his specific type of brain cancer. The results have been incredible and we're feeling hopeful. Several kids with the same type of tumor as our son have gone into full remission, so we're cautiously optimistic."

"The best kind of optimism to have." Thad smiled. He was still attempting to go full optimist like Emma, but some days were easier than others. "I've read the findings of the study you're talking about, and I think it's great you got Ricky a spot in the trials. He will hopefully do very well."

The clinical trial was the result of more than thirty years of research and used a viral immunotherapy injected directly into the patient's tumor, causing their own immune system to attack and destroy the cancer itself, without the use of harmful chemotherapy drugs. So far, they had a 90 percent response rate in pediatric patients with the same form of brain tumor as Ricky had, and the overall survival rate of the children in the study had more than doubled.

"And how do you feel about the trial, Ricky?" Emma asked, crouching to put herself at eye level while still holding Thad's hand.

"I'm just glad my parents aren't so worried anymore." Ricky glanced up at his mom and dad, who were smiling and looked happy. "I try to tell them that I'll be okay no matter what, but then they cry, so…" He shrugged, his knit hat crooked on his bald head. "Anyway, I don't want to talk about that stuff. Tonight's all about fun!" He hugged Emma around the neck, then pointed at a nearby booth. "Can we get some cotton candy, please? And then I want to go on the Ferris wheel with all my friends from the PICU. This is the best night of my life!"

He ran off to play with his friends and Emma straightened, sliding her arm around Thad's waist and hugging him tight. "We're both really thrilled for you and Ricky with the new trial. He's a strong kid with a great attitude. That will take him far in life."

"Thanks," Ricky's mom said. "We hope so. And thank you both again for all of this. It's such a blessing to us and to all the other families of sick children here tonight. It helps take them away from their problems for a little while. And that's such an important thing. You really have given us all the merriest of holidays."

They spent the rest of the evening walking around the carnival they'd created greeting guests. shaking hands and treating each family like they were the most important people on the planet. Emma still had to pinch herself every so often to make sure all of this, and Thad, were real. There'd been such a transformation in her life in such a short time. Her life before him hadn't been bad at all. She'd had her work and her sister and plans for the future. But now she could see how much better it all was with Thad in their lives. It had nothing to do with his money and everything to do with the amazing person he was inside.

And speaking of amazing…

People continued to approach them as one group of families left and another arrived. Grateful families continued to thank them personally and Thad pushed further and further beyond his boundaries and his Grinch-like past to blossom before her eyes, chatting and playing with the kids, even picking some of the smaller ones up—with their parents' permission—to give them a friendly cuddle. He spent time discussing each child's condition with their parents and even offering information about medical studies he'd seen or giving them names of experts to contact about this or that. All trace of his previous coldness and awkwardness seemed to have vanished. Even with his colleagues he was more open and friendly. And when Emma's sister Karley showed up with a couple of her school friends, Thad greeted them with the same enthusiasm he had the other kids, talking and even cracking a couple of jokes. Emma was impressed. And more than a little smitten with her newfound ho-ho-holiday hunk. As Thad walked Karley's friend over to one of the game vendors, Karley sidled up to her sister.

"I like him," her sister said. "And I can tell you do."

"I do," Emma agreed, any denials about her feelings for Thad way behind her. She wasn't quite ready to say the L-word yet, but things here definitely headed that way. "I really, really do."

"Good. I'm glad."

"You are?"

"Yes. I didn't want you to be alone when I go off to Howard next fall. Now you won't be."

"You sound awfully sure about yourself." Emma nudged her sister with her shoulder as they stood side by side watching Thad. "It's not like we're committed or anything."

Karley scoffed. "Girl. I see how he looks at you. And that man adores you. He's not going anywhere."

"You think?" Heat prickled Emma's cheeks despite the snow still falling around them.

"I know. Maybe you should take him to Green-Wood. Meet the parents, after the holidays." Karley winked, then pulled away from her sister. "I'll go rescue him from my friends and send him back. Have fun tonight."

"You, too!" Emma called, feeling so blessed to have such a wonderful sister. She took a seat at a nearby table to wait for Thad's return. She should take Thad to the cemetery. It was a special place to her, and she wanted to share it with him. In fact, she'd ask him about it later, after they got home. They could write their secrets and add them to the collection. Hers? Well, she'd met her Prince Charming, disguised as a Grinch, and won him for her very own. Not such a secret, maybe, but still the one that made her heart sing this Christmas.

Woof!

"What the—" Emma barely had time to turn around before a familiar black Lab ran up out of nowhere to put his paws on her jeans-covered knees, his tongue lolling out of the side of his mouth. She laughed and scratched the dog behind the ears. "Hello there, Baxter. How'd you get here?"

"I had someone from the foundation staff stop by the town house to bring him," Thad said, strolling up to her table. "He could use the exercise and since I'll miss his nightly walk, I figured this would be as good a place as any for him to run around. Plus, the kids seem to love him."

"Of course they do," Emma said, snuffling his adorable doggy face. Usually it was verboten to distract a service dog from his work, but Baxter was off-duty tonight and it was Christmas Eve. He deserved a little fun, too. "Who's a good boy, huh? I think you are. Yes, I do. Aren't you, Baxter?"

"Having a good time?" Thad asked, straddling the bench on the other side of the table.

"The best time." She grinned over at him. "We should grab a couple extra hot dogs from the vendor over there for a treat for Baxter. If that's okay with you?"

She glanced over at Thad then, only to find him watching her. She wanted to ask him what he was thinking, but then Ricky Lynch and his parents walked by their table again. They were on their way from the carousel to the Ferris wheel, and she'd never seen the boy look happier. As they passed, Baxter pulled at his leash until Thad nodded and Emma let the dog go and run up to the boy, licking and nudging Ricky, who laughed and laughed until Thad finally collected the dog and brought him back to their table.

The rest of the night passed in a blur for Emma, caught up in more people wanting to thank her and Thad, or pet Baxter. It seemed like she'd talked to more people that night than she had in all her years in the ER. And not one person commented on Thad's old reputation as a Grinch. Nope. It seemed that had disappeared as quickly as footprints in the falling snow.

And when it was all over and only Thad and Emma were left in the arena as the vendors tore down their booths and carnival rides, Thad held out his hand. "Emma, would you ride the carousel with me?"

Heart swelling with joy, she gave him a dazzling smile. "Yes, of course."

He escorted her to the now-empty pavilion and claimed one of the carriages, large enough for both of them and Baxter. They rode around and around, holding hands and laughing, same as the kids had done earlier, as the dog barked happily.

When their magical ride ended, he leaned in to kiss her, whispering, "I'm so glad I found you, Emma Trudeau. I can't imagine my life without you now."

She blinked hard against her tears of happiness. "Me, too, Thad. Me, too."

They kissed, sweet and deep, before he pulled back slightly to say against her lips, "Should I buy this for the gardens in back of the town house?"

Emma laughed with delight. "Nah. Let's wait until Everett's better, then we can all celebrate together."

"Deal." Thad grinned, then kissed her again.

EPILOGUE

Early Christmas Day, one year later

AT THE SOUND of Emma's voice echoing up from the foyer downstairs, Thad turned from where he was working in his study. It was only 6:00 a.m. Emma never got up that early on her days off. Dammit, he wasn't done with what he was working on yet.

Still, he finished pulling on his Santa suit with Everett's help, then looked at himself in the mirror.

"Wish me luck," he said to his old friend. The man was improving every day and could now walk and talk and even carry out most of his butler duties the same as before. But Thad made it a point not to overwork the man anymore. Everett was no longer an employee. He was a treasured member of Thad's found family and was treated as such.

The older man shook his head as he met

Thad's gaze in the mirror. "None needed. Go get her."

Nerves on high alert, Thad went downstairs, waiting until he got to the first floor before uttering a somewhat subdued, "Ho, ho, ho!"

He felt ridiculous, but if it made his Emma smile, it was worth it.

"You know my sister's still sleeping, right?" She eyed him up and down from where she sat in the living room, her arms crossed over her red plaid flannel pj's and her baby bump showing ever so slightly beneath. "And what are you wearing?"

"I'm Santa," Thad said, adjusting the velvet bag over his shoulder. "And I'm doing my job. Delivering gifts. And yes, I know Karley's still asleep." She'd moved into the town house along with Emma. The sisters were a package deal, he'd learned. Now Karley stayed here whenever she wasn't at Howard University pursuing her premed degree.

Thad walked past Emma into the living room on the first floor to deposit his presents. Lots and lots of presents. Packages of various shapes and sizes, all brightly wrapped and now overflowing beneath the tree. It had cost him a small fortune to hire personal shoppers to scour the stores of New York to find everything on the list Emma had given him last month, but if you were willing to spend enough, a person could do most anything. And he was counting on her sister staying asleep for a good long while yet.

"Why would you do that?" She stood in the doorway, staring at him and looking befuddled. "You don't even like Christmas."

"Maybe I've changed my mind." He scanned the gifts, then frowned as "White Christmas" played on the town house's sound system for the millionth time. Okay. Perhaps he'd become overzealous when he'd turned on the Christmas tunes. And with the gifts. And the decorations. But hey. He had a lot of time to make up for. Thad straightened then, set his empty bag aside and shrugged. "Women aren't the only ones allowed to change their minds. Apparently I just needed to be reminded of the real meaning of the holiday."

"Oh, you needed that all right," she scoffed, eyeing him suspiciously. "You changed your mind about Christmas, huh? Why?"

"You."

"Me?" This time she laughed with a great deal of irony. "I changed your mind about Christmas?"

"You changed my mind about everything,

Emma. About life. My life. And the life I want with you."

"Aw. That's sweet." She crossed the room to stand next to him, staring at the tree. "But why now?"

"Because now I'm sure I'm ready to move on to the future. With you. And our little one."

She placed a hand over her stomach and smiled. "That is a pretty good reason."

He put his arm around her and drew her into his side. "Someone once told me Christmas Day was the most magical day of the year. A day when miracles can happen." He kissed her temple, then tucked her head beneath his chin. That Christmas magic had surely shone down on him last year. Brought him the gift of a new lease on life, a woman he loved, and a new, found family of his own. A future he never could have imagined before, too. "I love you, Emma. And I plan to spend the rest of my life proving to you how much. You and our baby. Every single day."

He'd been so miserable before she'd arrived in his life. A fool. He'd pushed everyone away out of fear. Fear of feeling again. Fear of loving and losing. Fear of feeling, because with feeling came the risk of pain.

But you had to overcome those fears, had

to risk that pain, had to risk rejection, because the alternative wasn't acceptable. He took her hand and pulled a small blue box from the pocket of his Santa suit. This one didn't go beneath the tree, because if all went well, it would end up on her finger.

He got down on one knee and Emma put a trembling hand to her mouth. "What are you doing?"

"I've loved you from the first moment I saw you here in my kitchen, looking like an angel, Emma. And I want you by my side for as long as you'll have me. Please give me the chance to be the man you deserve." He swallowed hard and opened the box to reveal the sparkling diamond-and-platinum engagement ring. "Will you marry me?"

Tears trickled from her lovely eyes as she nodded. "Yes, Thad. I will marry you. I love you, too."

He slid the ring onto her finger, then stood to take her into his arms and kiss her soundly.

Emma didn't think she'd ever seen so many presents in her life.

Sitting on the floor, she picked up a box, shook it prior to carefully unwrapping it to reveal a beautiful aqua-colored baby blanket. He'd bought gifts for their baby. And now she was crying all over again. Running her fingers over the soft fuzzy material. "This is so beautiful."

"I'm glad you like it." He handed her another box. They repeated the process until she was surrounded with baby items. Some pink. Some blue. Some a mixture of pastels. They didn't know what they were having, wanting to be surprised for the first one.

Karley and Everett were in the dining room, playing a spirited game of Scrabble, and Baxter was happily enjoying his new toys in the corner. Their little family was happy and content.

"Wow. You've been busy." Emma bit her lip, taking it all in. "When did you have time to shop?"

"I had help, but don't hold that against me." He glanced at the two in the dining room, then gave a crooked grin. "Even Santa utilizes elves."

"Uh-huh," she said, knowing her sister and Everett had probably shopped for most of this, given her fiancé's busy work schedule these days. He was still as in demand as ever, though he'd cut back considerably on his hours, preferring to spend more time at home when he could. Still, it was sweet he'd thought of her and the baby and she loved all the gifts she'd gotten, even if she did feel bigger and more awkward each passing day. "Thank you, sweetie. I love everything."

Emma met his gaze and her breath caught at the intensity there, the vulnerability in his icy blue eyes. No protective walls. No barriers. Those were gone now, leaving only the man she loved with all her heart.

The music changed to "Have Yourself a Merry Little Christmas." Their song, the one they'd danced to last year at the fundraiser for the first time. Then it had been bittersweet for her. Now it was all goodness and light. Because this year, they would have a merry little Christmas. Together.

Thad held her close as they swayed slowly, his gaze reflecting back to her the same emotions she felt inside— love, gratitude, affection, desire. "I didn't think I'd ever feel this way about another person, Emma. Sometimes I wondered if I could love someone at all. But I do love you, my darling. More than I could ever say. Always and forever. And I can't wait to meet our baby."

"I love you, too." She wrapped her arms around him and kissed him, pulling back to laugh when their baby kicked hard between them. "I'd say our child shares our sentiments."

"Agreed." Thad grinned. "Merry Christmas, wife-to-be."

"Merry Christmas, husband-to-be," she said, cuddling into him again as the music switched to "It's the Most Wonderful Time of the Year." Corny, absolutely. But as Andy Williams warbled away in the background, Emma also knew it was true. This holiday was wonderful. The best ever for her. Knowing no matter what the future held, she and Thad and their family would face it together, for the rest of their lives.

* * * * *

*If you enjoyed this story, check out
these other great reads from
Traci Douglass*

Island Reunion with the Single Dad
Their Barcelona Baby Bombshell
Costa Rican Fling with the Doc
Her One-Night Secret

All available now!